the
Grandma's Attic
Storybook

Arleta Richardson

Chariot Books™
David C. Cook Publishing Co.

You'll enjoy all the books in
Arleta Richardson's Grandma's Attic Series:

Chariot Books™ is an imprint of Chariot Family Publishing
Cook Communications Ministries, Elgin, Illinois 60120
Cook Communications Ministries, Paris, Ontario
Kingsway Communications, Eastbourne, England

THE GRANDMA'S ATTIC STORYBOOK
© 1993 by Arleta Richardson for text

Designed by Dawn Lauck
Illustrated by Dora Leder
Illustration on page 252 by Susan Jerde
First Printing, 1992
Printed in the United States of America
97 96 95 94 5 4 3

Library of Congress Cataloging-in-Publication Data
Richardson, Arleta.
      The grandma's attic storybook / by Arleta Richardson.
             p.   cm.– (Grandma's attic series)
      Summary: As she listens to her grandmother's stories about her
childhood on the family farm in Michigan, a young girl learns some important
lessons about kindness, compassion, and the importance of prayer.
      ISBN 0-7814-0070-8
      [1. Country life – Fiction. 2. Grandmothers – Fiction 3. Christian life –
Fiction. 4. Michigan – Fiction.] I. Title. II. Series: Richardson, Arleta. Grandma's
attic series.
PZ7.R3942Gr 1993
[Fic]–dc20
                                     92–33823
                                          CIP
                                          AC

contents

She Loved to Tell a Story

HAVE YOU EVER WONDERED what life was like when your grandmother was a little girl? I did. And I was fortunate enough to have a grandma who could make stories come alive. She never forgot the fun and laughter of her childhood years.

I wish you could have known Grandma. You would have loved her. She was born one hundred years ago on a little farm in Michigan where she lived with her ma and pa and her two brothers, Reuben and Roy.

I never saw the little log house where Grandma was born, but I can imagine how it looked. It had one big room that was warmed by a fireplace and a big cookstove. Her brothers slept in a loft overhead, and Grandma slept in a trundle-bed beside her parents. (That is a little cot that slides under the big bed during the day.) The cabin sat in a small clearing in the woods, and even though there were no neighbors near, the family felt safe and protected in their little home. By the time Grandma was ready to go to school, the log cabin had been replaced by the big farmhouse that still stood when I was a little girl.

My trips to Grandma's old house were my favorite times. I explored from the attic to the root cellar, from the barn to the meadow brook—all places a little girl named Mabel, my grandma, knew and loved.

The attic was dusty and creaky, but what marvelous treasures it contained! A funny-looking wire thing that turned out to be something to wear. A slate and the hard pencil that Grandma used to write on it, and an ancient trunk filled with quilt pieces that Grandma and I put together for my bed.

The barn was still there, too, with lots more interesting things to look at. Nellie's harness hanging behind the stall. The buggy that Grandma had lost! An old door leaning up against the wall. A big rusty hook that sent Grandpa flying out over the barn floor.

From the dusty old attic to the front parlor with its slippery furniture, Grandma's old house was a storybook just waiting to be opened. I was fortunate to have a grandma who knew just how to open it. She loved to tell a story just as much as I loved to hear one.

And from my grandma I learned the meaning of kindness and compassion. I learned how important prayer is, and how rewarding life can be when it is lived for the Lord.

So if you are young enough to appreciate a story—and just about everyone is—come with me to a little farm in Michigan and enjoy the laughter and tears that old farmhouse saw so many years ago. . . .

Arleta Richardson

Arleta Richardson

chapter one

Pride Goes Before a Fall

"Grandma, what is this?"

Grandma looked up from her work.

"Good lands, child, where did you find that?"

"In the attic," I replied. "What is it, Grandma?"

Grandma chuckled and answered, "That's a hoop. The kind ladies wore under their skirts when I was a little girl."

"Did you ever wear one, Grandma?" I asked.

Grandma laughed. "Indeed I did," she said. "In fact, I wore that very one."

Here, I decided, must be a story. I pulled up the footstool and prepared to listen. Grandma looked at the old hoop fondly. . . .

◆

I ONLY WORE IT ONCE, but I kept it to remind me how painful pride can be.

I was about eight years old when that hoop

came into my life. For months I had been begging Ma to let me have a hoop skirt like the big girls wore. Of course, that was out of the question. What would a little girl, not even out of calicos, be doing with a hoop skirt? Nevertheless, I could envision myself walking haughtily to school with a hoop skirt and having all the girls watching enviously as I took my seat in the front of the room.

This dream was shared by my best friend and seatmate, Sarah Jane. Together we spent many hours picturing ourselves as fashionable young ladies in ruffles and petticoats. But try as we would, we could not come up with a single plan for getting a hoop skirt of our very own.

Finally, one day in early spring, Sarah Jane met me at the school grounds with exciting news. An older cousin had come to their house to visit, and she had two old hoops that she didn't want any longer. Sarah Jane and I could have them to play with, she said. Play with indeed! Little did that cousin know that we didn't want to play with them! Here was the answer to our dreams. All day, under cover of our books, Sarah Jane and I planned how we would wear those hoops to church on Sunday.

There was a small problem. How would I get that hoop into the house without Ma knowing about it? And how could either of us get out of

the house with them on when no one could see us? It was finally decided that I would stop by Sarah Jane's house on Sunday morning. We would have some excuse for walking to church, and after her family had left, we would put on our hoops and prepare to make a grand entrance at the church.

"Be sure to wear your fullest skirt." Sarah Jane reminded me. "And be here early. They're all sure to look at us this Sunday!" If we had only known how true that would be! But of course, we were happily unaware of the disaster that lay ahead.

Sunday morning came at last, and I astonished my family by the speed with which I finished my chores and was ready to leave for church.

"I'm going with Sarah Jane this morning." I announced, and set out quickly before there was any protest.

All went according to plan. Sarah Jane's family went on in the buggy cautioning us to hurry, and not be late for service. We did have a bit of trouble fastening the hoops around our waists and getting our skirts pulled down to cover them. But when finally we were ready, we agreed that there could not be two finer looking young ladies in the county than we were.

Quickly we set out for church, our fine hoop skirts swinging as we walked. Everyone had gone in when we arrived, so we were assured of the grand entry we desired. Proudly, with small noses tipped up, we sauntered to the front of the church and took our seats.

Alas! No one had ever told us the hazards of sitting down in a hoop skirt without careful practice! The gasps we heard were not of admiration as we had anticipated—far from it! For when we sat down, those dreadful hoops flew straight up in the air! Our skirts covered our faces, and the startled minister was treated to the sight of two pairs of white pantalettes and flying petticoats.

Sarah Jane and I were too startled to know how to disentangle ourselves, but our mothers were not. Ma quickly snatched me from the seat and marched me out the door.

The trip home was a silent one. My dread grew with each step. What terrible punishment would I receive at the hands of an embarrassed and upset parent? Although I didn't dare look at her, I knew she was upset because she was shaking. It was to be many years before I learned that Ma was shaking from laughter, and not from anger!

Nevertheless, punishment was in order. My Sunday afternoon was spent with the big Bible and Pa's concordance. My task was to copy each verse I could find that had to do with being proud. It was a sorry little girl who learned a lesson about pride going before a fall that day.

The story was ended.

"And you were never proud again, Grandma?" I asked.

Grandma thought soberly for a moment. "Yes," she replied. "I was proud again. Many times. It was not until I was a young lady and the Lord saved me, that I had the pride taken from my heart. But many times when I am tempted to be proud, I remember that horrid hoop skirt, and decide that a proud heart is an abomination to the Lord!"

chapter two

Grandma's Sampler

"Something is wrong with this, Grandma," I said. "It doesn't have as many stitches as I started out with."

Grandma took my knitting and looked at it carefully.

"You dropped a stitch back here," she said, and using a crochet hook, she worked the missing stitch back up to the needle.

"It's easier to pick up a stitch as soon as it's dropped than it is to go back and get it later. Sometimes you have to take your work out all the way back to the mistake."

Grandma handed the knitting back to me and picked up her own work. "I remember that I never had much patience with doing things over when I was your age. In fact, one time I decided not to bother, and I was sorry about it afterward."

"Were you knitting something?" I asked.

"No," Grandma replied. "It was a sampler I was embroidering. It was in the spring, just before school was out. . . .

13

THE TEACHER HAD ANNOUNCED early in the year that there would be a contest. Everyone in the room would enter some kind of handwork to be judged by the school board members the last day of school. The prize would be a book—and we didn't have many books of our own.

I determined that I would win the prize, and announced my intentions at the supper table the very day we found out about the contest. "I'm going to have a new book the last day of school," I said to the family.

"You are?" Pa said. "Are you saving all your money to get one?"

Pa knew that I didn't have any money, or any prospects of getting any, so I knew he was just fooling.

I shook my head. "No, I'll get a new book for winning the contest for the best handwork."

"What makes you think you'll win?" Roy asked. "I'm going to enter the contest too, you know."

"Yes, but I'm a more carefuller worker than you are," I replied.

"You mean 'a more careful' worker," Ma corrected me. Then she eyed me thoughtfully. "On the other hand, you aren't the most careful worker I've ever seen."

"I will be this time," I said confidently. "I won't hurry, and I'll take lots of pains to do it just right. And besides, I already prayed about it. I asked God to let me win."

This seemed to settle the matter for me. Since I knew the Lord answered prayer, I had no question about winning. Even when Pa reminded me that God wasn't going to do the work for me, I was still sure I would win.

The next day Sarah Jane and I decided that we would enter the sewing division and make a sampler. Between our two homes we would surely find enough bright-colored thread to work with, and a square of white linen was not hard to come by.

"What are you going to say on yours?" Sarah Jane asked.

"I haven't decided yet," I replied. "What are you putting on yours?"

"I think I'll put 'Home is where the heart is' and make a border of hearts and flowers. Doesn't that sound pretty?"

"Yes, it does," I said. "I think I'd like something about friends on mine."

"How about 'A friend loveth at all times'?" Sarah Jane suggested. "That was our Bible verse last week."

"That's good. I'll use that. We'd better practice

on something else first though. The one for the contest has to be perfect."

Sarah Jane agreed, and we began drawing the patterns for our letters and flowers. When we finally had them just right, we carefully transferred the work to the cloth.

In the weeks that followed we used every spare moment we had to embroider our samplers. I did the border first, with little flowers and leaves, and I thought it looked quite pretty. Ma agreed.

"You are doing better than I expected, Mabel," she said. "If you do as well on the words, you may have a chance at winning that book."

"Of course I'll win, Ma! Sarah Jane's looks nice, but it's not as smooth as mine. She said so herself."

"Just don't be disappointed if you aren't first," Ma warned. "It doesn't pay to be too sure of yourself."

But I was sure of myself. I just knew that mine was going to be the best one.

About two weeks before the end of the term, Sarah Jane and I sat on the porch, working on our samplers.

"I have just two more words to do, then my name and the date," I announced, and I spread the sampler out on my lap to inspect it again. Sarah Jane looked at it carefully; then an odd expression came over her face.

"Something is wrong, Mabel," she said.

"There can't be!" I exclaimed. "What is it?"

"I think you spelled friend wrong."

Horrified, I looked at the word. Sure enough, I had written "A FREND LOVETH AT . . ."

"Oh, no! What can I do to fix it up?"

"You'll have to take it out, back to there," Sarah Jane said. "There isn't room to squeeze an i in without looking funny."

"But I don't have time to take it all out," I cried. "Besides it will leave holes where I sewed it, and that will look worse!"

Sarah Jane was sorry, and so was I. It was either take the stitching all out, and probably not finish in time, or leave it in and hope the judges wouldn't notice, but I knew I wouldn't win.

Ma was sympathetic. "I think you should put an i in here, even though it looks crowded. That would be better than having the judges believe you thought it was spelled correctly. As many times as you've looked at that sampler, I can't understand how you missed it."

"That's what Sarah Jane said, too," I replied sadly. "When I looked at it, I just thought how pretty it was. I wasn't expecting anything to be wrong. I did so want to win that book! I was sure the Lord would answer my prayers."

"Maybe you should have prayed to do your best rather than to win, Mabel. The Lord is willing to help us, but we need to do all we can with the intelligence he gave us."

I knew Ma was right, but I was pretty sad the day I took the sampler to school. The teacher agreed that if it hadn't been for that mistake, it might have been a winner.

The last day of school was exciting, anyway. When the contest winners were announced, Roy was in first place in the wood-carving division with a small squirrel he had whittled.

"You can be the first one to read my book, Mabel," he offered generously. "Maybe next year you can enter again and win your own prize."

"That was a good lesson for me," Grandma said. "I was often careless after that, but I was careful not to be quite so positive about what I would do again. And I never blamed the Lord for my mistakes, either!"

chapter three

Charlotte

"Grandma," I wailed, "look what happened to Virginia!" I held up my doll so Grandma could see how her leg had come away from her body. "Can she be fixed?"

Grandma examined the doll carefully. "I should think so. I imagine your Uncle Roy can mend her. Ask him when he comes in from the barn."

I sat on the steps and waited for Uncle Roy. As soon as he appeared I rushed to meet him.

"Grandma says you can fix Virginia, Uncle Roy. Will you try, please?"

Uncle Roy sat down and looked at the dangling leg. "I think a new piece of wire will take care of that. I'll fix it for you right after dinner."

He turned the doll over and laughed. "They sure don't make dolls like they used to. I remember a doll baby your Grandma had."

"Was it Emily?" I asked.

"Mercy," Uncle Roy replied, "I don't know what she called it. I remember that I called it a mess—and so did Ma."

At the dinner table that night, I questioned Grandma. "What doll did you have that your mother and Uncle Roy thought was a mess?"

Grandma thought for a moment. "You must mean Charlotte. I'd almost forgotten about her. How did you remember, Roy?"

"I was with you when you found it," Uncle Roy said. "I tried to discourage you from taking it home, but you wouldn't listen to me."

"That's right. You were there, weren't you? I wonder why Ma ever let me into the house with it."

"Because you were spoiled," Uncle Roy said and he winked at me.

"What was the matter with it?" I asked. "Why shouldn't you bring it into the house?"

"Well," Grandma said, "it was a mess. No one in the family had anything good to say about it. But I thought any doll was lovable."

"Where did you find it?" I asked.

Grandma got up to clear the table and began the story. . . .

H

IT WAS A RAINY SPRING DAY in my first year of school. Roy and I were walking home together through the woods. I was lagging behind, as usual, and Roy had stopped to tell me to hurry up. He didn't particularly like his little sister tagging along, but he was responsible for me, so he didn't dare let me out of his sight.

"Come on, Mabel," he said. "You can walk faster than that. I've got chores to do before I can play. Just because you never have to do anything. . . ."

"I do so!" I retorted. "I help Ma set the table, and I dry the knives and forks."

Roy snorted and turned to walk on.

"Wait a minute, Roy. Look at this."

Reluctantly he came back to where I stood. "Well, what is it?"

I bent over to pick something out of the mud. It was a doll—soaked almost beyond recognition. The features were nearly gone, and the clothes were torn and dripping. But to my motherly eye, it was beautiful. I hugged it to me as Roy watched in disgust.

"Ugh!" he groaned. "Throw it back! That's awful! Wait until Ma sees what you've gotten all over your front!"

I looked down and saw that I had ruined my dress; mud and water were soaking through my apron. I knew that Ma would not be pleased about that, but I couldn't throw the doll back.

"I'll take it home and clean it up," I said. "See,

I'll hold it way out here." I held the doll at arm's length and began to run for home.

"It's too late to hold it way out there," Roy called after me. "You're already a mess. If I were you, I'd chuck that thing in the nearest hole."

I ignored him and continued on my way. When I ran into the kitchen, Ma was horrified.

"Oh, Mabel! What happened to you? Did you fall down? And what is that?"

"It's a doll, Ma. I found it in the woods and brought it home to take care of it. It just needs to be washed a little."

"It needs to be buried," Roy said. "I told her to leave it there, but she wouldn't listen." He put his lunch pail on the table.

"Where is your lunch pail, Mabel?" Ma asked. "Did you leave it at school again?"

"No, I had it when I left school. I must have laid it down on the road when I stopped to pick up the doll."

Ma sighed. "Go back and get her lunch pail, Roy. I don't have anything else she can carry her lunch in."

"Oh, Ma! Why can't she go back for it? It's her pail!"

Ma looked at Roy. "I guess I can put her lunch in with yours. You'll have to eat with her tomorrow."

"I'll go. I'll go."

"And you," Ma said to me, "take that filthy thing out and wash it in the trough. Then come back and change your clothes."

I knew then that Ma would let me keep the doll, but I didn't know what a surprise was in store for us. I hurried outside and swished it around in the water until most of the mud was gone, then brought it back to the kitchen.

"She's awfully heavy, Ma, but I couldn't get any more water out."

"Put it on the back of the stove to dry. And change your dress. You're a sight."

When Reuben came in with a load of wood, he poked a finger into the doll. "What's this?" he asked Ma.

"It's Mabel's doll. She found it on the way home from school."

"What's it stuffed with—rocks?"

"It's waterlogged," Ma replied. "It won't be that stiff when it dries out."

By the time Pa came in for supper, the doll had begun to smell musty.

"Phew!" Pa's face twisted in mock disgust. "What smells like an old burlap bag? I hope it's not what we're having for supper."

"Hardly," Ma answered. "It's Mabel's doll. It will probably take all night to dry out."

Several more comments were made about that

doll before I went to bed: Roy offered it a decent burial, and Reuben declared he wouldn't touch it with a stick. Pa thought he'd better sit on the porch after supper and air out, since he smelled like a burlap bag himself after sitting by the stove.

I didn't think any of them were very funny. "Ma, you won't let anyone touch my doll, will you?"

"No, of course not. You get on to bed now."

"I'm going to name her Charlotte. Don't you think that's a pretty name?"

"Lovely. Now go to bed."

Sometime later that evening, Pa and the boys were sitting in the kitchen. Pa was reading and the boys were doing their homework. Ma came in and found Reuben staring strangely at the stove.

"Ma, something's the matter with that doll."

"Is it burning?" Ma said as she ran over to the stove.

"No, but I think it's alive!"

Pa looked up from his book. "Thy learning is turning thee mad," he teased.

"He's crazy," Roy added.

Nevertheless they all stared at the doll. Suddenly an arm jerked up; then one of the legs kicked out. Ma jumped back from the stove.

"Mercy! What's going on?"

As they watched, the doll became more lively.

The head bobbed, and the arms and legs flopped wildly.

"Throw it on the floor!" Pa ordered.

"Jump on it!" Roy shouted.

Ma gingerly picked up the doll and dropped it on the table, where it continued to toss and turn in a most lifelike way.

"At least it's beginning to smell better," Reuben said. "It smells almost like popcorn!"

"It is popcorn!" Ma exclaimed. "That's what it's stuffed with."

And sure enough, that's exactly what was in it. After the doll stopped jumping, Ma ripped it open and dumped out the corn.

Pa looked at the mess distastefully. "That old rag isn't worth stuffing again, is it?"

"No," Ma admitted, "it isn't. But I promised Mabel I wouldn't let anyone touch her doll, so I'll have to put something in it."

"Fill it with catnip," Reuben suggested. "Maybe the cat will drag it off and lose it."

"Naw," said Roy. "Put pepper in it. Then Mabel will be glad to get rid of it."

But Ma was more sympathetic. "If this old rag makes Mabel happy, then she can have it. I'll wash it up and fill it with rice."

And that's what she did. I played with Charlotte for a long while. . . .

Grandma looked at my doll, which Uncle Roy had mended as he listened to the story. "You're right. They don't make dolls like they used to."

chapter four

Mrs. Carter's Fright

"Grandma, you never told me you dressed a pig in baby's clothes! What did you do that for?" I asked, wondering why my common sense grandma would do such a thing, even when she was a little girl like me.

"Oh, my friend Sarah Jane and I should have been whipped for that prank! We frightened poor Mrs. Carter nearly out of her senses. If she hadn't been such a kind, forgiving lady, I'm sure we would have been punished severely."

"Tell me what happened, Grandma," I begged.

"After I get the bread in the oven, we'll sit on the porch. You can help me pick over the beans for supper."

Soon we were seated on the porch, and Grandma began. . . .

THIS STORY HAPPENED RIGHT ON THIS PORCH. At least, most of it did. It was a beautiful day in the spring, shortly after school was over for the year. Sarah Jane and I were wandering about, trying to think of the best way to spend the day. We had about decided on a trip to the woods to look for berries when Ma changed our minds.

"Don't go too far from the house, girls," she called. "Mrs. Carter is coming to spend the day sewing, and she's bringing her new baby. I know you'll want to see her."

Of course we did. There weren't a lot of new babies in our community, and Sarah Jane and I both loved them. We even thought Mrs. Carter might let us play with little Lucy. So we hung around the gate and watched the road for the first sight of the Carter's wagon.

Very soon it appeared, and we watched Mr. Carter drive up to the front porch. After helping Mrs. Carter down from the front seat, he went to the back of the wagon and took out a beautiful baby buggy. Sarah Jane and I had never seen one so fine before.

"Oh, Mrs. Carter," I said, "may we push Lucy around in the buggy?"

"We'll be very, very careful," Sarah Jane chimed in.

Mrs. Carter smiled at us. "I don't know why not. Just don't go too far from the house. She should go to sleep soon; then you can put the buggy here in the shade, close to the porch."

She laid the baby down, and after admiring her for a few minutes, we began to push the buggy slowly around the yard.

"Wouldn't it be fun to have a real baby to take care of?" I said.

"Oh, yes!" Sarah Jane replied. "Our dolls are nice, but they don't move around and cry like a baby does."

After what seemed like a very short time, the baby went to sleep. We took a few more turns around the house and even shook the buggy a little to see if she might wake up. Finally we decided to put the buggy in the shade as Mrs. Carter had told us to. Then we sat on the edge of the porch and admired the pretty dress and bonnet the baby wore.

"She looks just like a little doll, doesn't she?" Sarah Jane said. "Your doll, Emily, is just about that size. Shall we get our dolls and play with them?"

I agreed, and we brought our dolls and doll clothes back out to the porch where we could watch the baby as she slept. After a few minutes, Sarah Jane tired of the dolls.

"I'd rather dress something that moves a little," she said, and then spotting the cat walking across the yard, she suggested, "Maybe we could dress the cat."

"You might be able to put clothes on your cat," I said, "but you'll never get a dress and bonnet on this one. He's awfully particular about what he does."

"I suppose Pep wouldn't like it either," Sarah Jane said, figuring our dog was the next best choice.

"I'm sure of it," I replied. "Besides, his head is too big to fit this bonnet."

We sat for a few moments longer, swinging our feet back and forth, when suddenly a brilliant thought came to me.

"I know! how about one of the new baby pigs in the barn? All they do is sleep, but at least they're alive. Shall we get one?"

"Oh, yes, let's!" Sarah Jane exclaimed. "That would be just right for the doll clothes."

So we hurried out to the barn to pick out the cleanest, pinkest piglet we could find. Sure enough, when we had put the dress on that pig and tied the bonnet under its chin, we had what we thought was the next best thing to a real baby.

"Isn't that cute?" Sarah Jane said. "We should have thought of this before." She eyed the buggy, which little Lucy was sleeping in. "I think we should take our baby for a ride."

"We can't put the pig in with Mrs. Carter's baby!" I protested. "She wouldn't like that. Besides,

Lucy's still asleep. We might wake her up."

Sarah Jane thought that over. "Why don't you put the baby on your bed to sleep while we take the pig for a ride? Mrs. Carter wouldn't care if you did that."

"OK, she'll be comfortable there." I lifted the baby carefully from the buggy, and with Sarah Jane opening the doors for me, I tiptoed quietly up to my room and put Lucy down on my bed.

"You'd better put her right in the middle so she won't roll off," Sarah Jane suggested.

"She's not big enough to roll over," I said, but I put her as close to the center of the bed as I could and covered her with a blanket. Then we tiptoed out and closed the door.

"There," Sarah Jane said. "She'll probably sleep all morning. Let's take the pig for a ride."

So we ran back outside, put the pig in the buggy, and covered it with a doll blanket. It promptly fell asleep, and we had a great time pretending to be fine ladies strolling through town with their beautiful baby.

Very shortly Ma came to the kitchen door. "Girls, it would be nice if you would run to the woods and gather some berries for dinner. It won't be long until it's time to eat. Is the baby still asleep?"

"Yes, Ma." I replied. "She's asleep."

"Good. Be sure to leave the buggy in the shade. This small bucket should hold enough berries," she said as she handed us a container.

There was nothing for us to do but take the bucket and start for the woods.

"We'd better hurry," I said, realizing what might happen if we were gone too long.

We picked the berries as fast as we could, not even stopping to eat a few now and then as we always did. Still it seemed as though the bucket would never fill up. At last we had enough and started back to the house.

As soon as we reached the clearing and could see the house, we knew we were in trouble.

"Oh, no!" Sarah Jane cried as we surveyed the scene before us.

Everyone seemed to be in motion. Roy was galloping toward the woods where we stood. Reuben was racing for the barn, carrying something that looked like a small pig in doll clothes, and Pep was running between the two of them, not sure whom to follow. The only still figures were Mrs. Carter, who was lying on the porch steps, and Ma, who was kneeling beside her, wiping her friend's face with a cloth.

"I think they've found the pig," Sarah Jane observed.

I nodded.

"We'd better get moving," Sarah Jane said. "We're in for it sooner or later!"

By this time, Roy had reached us, and he breathlessly reported the news. "Someone stole Mrs. Carter's baby and left a pig in the buggy. You're going to get it, because it's wearing your doll clothes."

"I told you Lucy would sleep for hours," Sarah Jane declared impatiently. "She didn't even cry to let them know where she was. How did we know they'd look for her before she woke up?"

I was sure that argument wasn't going to impress Ma, because I had used similar logic on her before without success. But the sooner they found out where the baby was, the better off we would be.

Once everyone stopped long enough to listen, Sarah Jane and I explained everything, and Mrs. Carter was reunited with her baby. When she saw that Lucy was safe, she told Ma not to punish us.

"They just didn't think. I know they didn't mean to be bad."

"They'd better learn to think," Ma replied crossly.

"Do you suppose you can ring the dinner bell without doing something foolish?" she said to me.

Soon Pa came in from the field and washed for dinner. Sarah Jane and I sat as quietly as we could, hoping that no one would pay any attention to us and praying that the boys wouldn't tell Pa what had happened.

Unfortunately they didn't need to. Pa sat down, asked the blessing, and looked around the table. "Would someone tell me what the fool pig is doing down in the pen with doll rags on? The sow won't even let it come near her." Pa waited for someone to reply.

Sarah Jane and I avoided his glance, Roy sputtered into his glass, and Reuben looked disgusted. Then, to our surprise, Ma and Mrs. Carter began to laugh!

Pa laughed too, when he heard the story, making Sarah Jane and I feel better. . . .

▦

Grandma picked up the pan of beans and went to check on her bread. I sat on the steps and looked out over the front yard. I could almost see the buggy and that funny pig!

chapter five

The Nuisance in Ma's Kitchen

When Grandma called from the backyard, I knew I was in for it. It was her would-you-look-at-this voice, which usually meant I was responsible for something.

"What, Grandma?" I asked, once I reached where she was hanging up the washing.

"Would you look at this? I just went into the kitchen for more clothespins, and came back out to find this."

I looked where she was pointing. One of my kittens had crawled into the clothes basket and lay sound asleep on a clean sheet.

"If you're going to have kittens around the house, you'll have to keep an eye on them. Otherwise, leave them in the barn where they belong. It's hard enough to wash sheets once without doing them over again."

Grandma headed toward the house with the soiled sheet, and I took the kitten back to the barn. But I didn't agree that it belonged there. I would much rather have had the whole family of kittens in the house with me.

Later I mentioned this to Grandma.

"I know," she said. "I felt the same way when I was your age. If it had been up to me, I would have moved every animal on the place into the house every time it rained or snowed."

"Didn't your folks let any pets in the house?" I asked.

"Most of our animals weren't pets," Grandma admitted. "But there were a few times when they were allowed in. If an animal needed special care, it stayed in the kitchen. I really enjoyed those times, especially if it was one I could help with."

"Tell me about one," I said, encouraging her to tell me another story about her childhood.

"I remember one cold spring when Pa came in from the barn carrying a tiny goat . . .

田

"I'M NOT SURE WE CAN SAVE THIS ONE." Pa held the baby goat up for us to see. "The nanny had twins last night, and she'll only let one come near her. I'm afraid this one's almost gone."

Ma agreed and hurried to find an old blanket and a box for a bed. She opened the oven door, put the box on it, and gently took the little goat and laid it on the blanket. It didn't move at all, just lay there barely breathing.

"Oh, Ma," I said. "Do you think it will live? Shouldn't we give it something to eat?"

37

"It's too weak to eat right now," Ma replied. "Let it rest and get warm, then we'll try to feed it."

Fortunately it was Saturday, and I didn't have to go to school. I sat on the floor next to the oven and watched the goat. Sometimes it seemed as though it had stopped breathing, and I would call Ma to look.

"It's still alive," she assured me. "It just isn't strong enough to move yet. You sit there and watch if you want to, but don't call me again unless it opens its eyes."

When Pa and my brothers came in for dinner, Reuben stopped and looked down at the tiny animal. "Doesn't look like much, does it?"

I burst into tears. "It does so!" I howled. "It looks just fine! Ma says it's going to open its eyes. Don't discourage it!"

Reuben backed off in surprise, and Pa came over to comfort me. "Now, Reuben wasn't trying to harm that goat. He just meant that it doesn't . . . look like a whole lot."

I started to cry again, and Ma tried to soothe me. "Crying isn't going to help that goat one bit," she said. "When it gets stronger, it will want something to eat. I'll put some milk on to heat while we have dinner."

I couldn't leave my post long enough to go to the table, so Ma let me hold my plate in my lap. I ate dinner watching the goat. Suddenly it quivered and opened its mouth.

"It's moving, Ma!" I shouted. "You'd better bring the milk!"

Ma soaked a rag in the milk, and I held it while the little goat ate greedily. By the time it had fallen asleep again, I was convinced that it would be just fine.

And it was. By evening the little goat was standing on its wobbly legs and began to baa loudly for more to eat.

"Pa, maybe you'd better bring its box into my room," I suggested at bedtime.

"Whatever for?" Pa asked. "It will keep warm right here by the stove. We'll look after it during the night. Don't worry."

"And we aren't bringing your bed out here," Ma added, anticipating my next suggestion. "You'll have enough to do, watching that goat during the day."

Of course, Ma was right. As the goat got stronger, he began to look for things to do. At first he was contented to grab anything within reach and pull it. Dish towels, apron strings, and tablecloth corners all fascinated him. I was kept busy trying to move things out of his way.

From the beginning the little goat took a special liking to Ma, but she was not flattered.

"I can't move six inches in this kitchen without stumbling over that animal," she sputtered. "He can be sound asleep in his box one minute and sitting on my feet the next. I don't know how much longer I can tolerate him in here."

As it turned out, it wasn't much longer. The next Monday Ma prepared to do the washing in the washtub Pa had placed on two chairs near the woodpile. Ma always soaked the clothes in cold water first, then transferred them to the boiler on the stove.

I was in my room when I heard her shouting. "Now you put that down! Come back here!"

I ran to the kitchen door and watched as the goat circled the table with one of Pa's shirts in his mouth. Ma was right behind him, but he managed to stay a few feet ahead of her.

"Step on the shirt, Ma!" I shouted as I ran into the room. "Then he'll have to stop!"

I started around the table the other way, hoping to head him off. But the goat seemed to realize that he was outnumbered, for he suddenly turned and ran toward the chairs that held the washtub.

"Oh, no!" Ma cried. "Not that way!"

But it was too late! Tub, water, and clothes splashed to the floor. The goat danced stiff-legged through the soggy mess with a surprised look on his face.

"That's enough!" Ma said. "I've had all I need

of that goat. Take him out and tie him in the yard, Mabel. Then bring me the mop, please."

I knew better than to say anything, but I was worried about what would happen to the goat. If he couldn't come back in the kitchen, where would he sleep?

Pa had the answer to that. "He'll go to the barn tonight."

"But Pa," I protested, "he's too little to sleep in the barn, besides, he'll think we don't like him anymore!"

"He'll think right," Ma said. "He's a menace, and he's not staying in my kitchen another day."

"But I like him," I replied. "I feel sorry for him out there alone. If he has to sleep in the barn, let me go out and sleep with him!"

My two brothers looked at me in amazement.

"You?" Roy exclaimed. "You won't even walk past the barn after dark, let alone go in!"

Everyone knew he was right. I had never been very brave about going outside after dark. But I was more concerned about the little goat than I was about myself.

"I don't care," I said stubbornly. "He'll be scared out there and he's littler than I am."

Ma didn't say anything, probably because she thought I'd change my mind before dark. I didn't though. When Pa started for the barn that evening,

I was ready to go with him. Ma saw that I was determined, so she brought me a blanket.

"You'd better wrap up in this," she said. "The hay is warm, but it's pretty scratchy."

I took the blanket and followed Pa and the goat out to the barn. The more I thought about the long, dark night, the less it seemed like a good idea, but I wasn't going to give in, or admit that I was afraid.

Pa found a good place for me to sleep. "This is nice and soft and out of the draft. You'll be fine here."

I rolled up in the blanket, hugging the goat close to me as I watched Pa check the animals. The light from the lantern cast long scary shadows through the barn, and I thought about asking Pa if he would stay with me. I knew better, though, and all too soon he was ready to leave.

"Good night, Mabel. Sleep well," he said as he closed the barn door behind him. I doubted that I would sleep at all. If it hadn't been for the goat and my brothers who would laugh at me, I would have returned to the house at once. Instead I closed my eyes tightly and began to say my prayers. In a few moments the barn door opened, and Reuben's voice called to me.

"Mabel," he said, "it's just me." He came over to where I lay, and I saw that he had a blanket under his arm.

"I thought I'd sleep out here tonight, too. I haven't slept in the barn for a long time. You don't mind, do you?"

"Oh, no. That's fine." I turned over and fell asleep at once.

When I awoke in the morning, the goat and Reuben were both gone. Soon I found the goat curled up by his mother.

"Will you be sleeping in the barn again tonight?" Ma asked me at breakfast.

"No, I don't think so," I said. "I'll take care of the goat during the day, but I guess his mother can watch him at night . . . ."

Grandma laughed at the memory. "After I grew up, I told Reuben how grateful I was that he came out to stay with me. I wonder how my family ever put up with all my foolishness."

Grandma went back into the house, and I wandered out to the barn to see the little kittens. I decided I wouldn't be brave enough to spend the night there— even with a big brother to keep me company!

chapter six

The Big Snow Storm

I pressed my nose against the kitchen window to watch the snow fall in big flakes past the glass.

"Do you think we will be snowed in, Grandma?" I asked.

Grandma came over and looked out the window. "Probably not. If the wind comes up tonight the snow may drift around the house, but it isn't deep enough to keep us snowbound. It doesn't seem to snow as much as it did when I was a little girl. I can remember walking on frozen snow as high as the fence tops."

"Really? I never saw that much snow. That must have been lots of fun!"

"It was, as long as you didn't hit a soft spot and fall in. Then you could be in snow over your head, and you'd need help to climb out."

"I wish it would do that again," I said. "I can't think of anything more fun than being snowed in."

"Well, I can think of a few things more fun,"

Grandma replied, "but there probably isn't anything much more exciting. There are a lot of things to take care of on a farm if you know you can't get out for a while. I remember one snow storm when things almost got out of hand around here. . . .

▦

IT WAS IN THE EARLY SPRING, and the ground had been clear for several weeks. We thought that winter was over, and it would soon be warm. One morning when it was still dark Pa came in from the barn.

"Boys," he said to Reuben and Roy, "I'll need your help after breakfast to get extra feed down for the animals. I smell a storm in the air."

"What does a storm smell like, Pa?" I asked him.

Pa looked puzzled. "I guess I can't tell you that. It's something you just know when you've lived in the country all your life."

"I've lived in the country all my life," I replied, "and I don't remember ever smelling a storm."

Roy looked at me in disgust. "What do you know about anything? You probably wouldn't know a storm if you got caught in it."

"I would so," I retorted. "I'm as smart as you are!"

"Enough," Pa said. "We've heard all this before. Let's eat and get to work."

46

After breakfast, Pa and the boys departed for the barn, and Ma and I started to clean up the kitchen. As it began to get light, I looked out the window. This day looked as nice as the ones before it.

"Pa must have smelled wrong," I said. "It's too nice to storm."

"He may have," Ma laughed, "but I wouldn't count on it. He's a pretty good weatherman."

As the morning wore on, it began to look as though Pa was going to be right. Clouds came in, and by dinner time it was almost as dark as evening.

"We'll get extra wood after dinner," Pa announced. "And it might be well to bring the rope from the barn."

I knew what that was for. Pa had a long, heavy rope that he tied to the barn door and stretched along the path to the kitchen door. In a heavy blizzard it was sometimes hard to see the barn from the house, and the rope was a guide to go out and feed the animals.

Before dinner was over, it had begun to snow hard. When they finished eating, Pa and the boys went back out. Ma hurriedly cleared the table, then put on her heavy sweater.

"I'm going to the cellar, Mabel," she said. "I think I'd better bring up some canned goods and vegetables before the snow covers the doors. Would you mind starting the dishes? I'll help as soon as I get back."

Ma took a large basket with her and opened the back door. Immediately it was pulled out of her hands and banged against the house.

"Mercy! Come and close the door, please, Mabel. This is turning into a real blizzard."

And indeed it was. After Ma left, I stood at the window and watched her struggle to get the cellar door open. She finally managed to get one side up, and apparently deciding that was enough, she disappeared into the cellar. I watched the storm for a few minutes, then reluctantly started the dishes.

Sometime later Pa came around the corner of the house, and seeing the cellar door open, muttered something about those careless boys, and closed the door. When he brought a load of wood into the kitchen, he stopped to warm his hands over the stove.

"Where's Ma?" he asked me.

"She went to get some vegetables. She said she'd be right back to help me with the dishes."

Pa nodded and went out again. He and the boys brought in load after load of wood; then they began to carry in water. Pa stopped again by the stove.

"What's the matter here? The fire is dying down. Where's Ma?"

"I told you, Pa," I answered. "She went to get some vegetables. She sure has been gone a long time. I've had to do all these dishes alone."

Suddenly Pa looked horrified. "Vegetables! You mean Ma went to the cellar for vegetables? Why didn't you say so?"

He dashed out the door and down the stairs to the cellar, leaving me saying "I thought you knew!" to an empty kitchen.

In a moment they were back, with Pa carrying the basket, and Ma rubbing her hands together and stamping the snow from her feet.

"That cellar is not the warmest place on the farm," she said. "I'd rather have been shut in the barn if you were going to leave me locked up all afternoon. I'll probably catch my death of foolishness."

And sure enough, by evening Ma was feverish and beginning to cough.

"I'm sorry, Maryanne," Pa said anxiously. "That was a terrible thing for me to do. I was in such a hurry I just didn't think."

"Don't worry about it," Ma said hoarsely. "It'll probably be just a slight cold. I'll get to bed early, and it will be all better by morning."

Unfortunately, Ma was wrong. By morning her

49

cold, and the storm, had worsened. When she decided to stay in bed, I realized that she was sicker than I had ever known her to be.

Pa and the boys were glad to have the rope when they went to milk and feed the animals, but they knew there was no chance of getting farther than the barn.

"As soon as the storm lets up, I'll go and get the doctor for Ma," Pa told us. "I guess you'll all have to help me keep things going until she's well."

Since everyone had to stay in the house, Pa didn't worry about the outside. His biggest problem seemed to be getting the meals.

"This always looks easy when Ma does it," he said to me the next morning. "Ask her how many cups of baking powder to put in the pancakes."

"Cups!" Ma croaked when I asked her. "Mercy on us! He'll kill us all with indigestion! Tell him two tablespoons to three cups of flour."

I was kept busy running between the kitchen and the bedroom for instructions. Finally, Ma suggested that he stick to things like meat and potatoes and other vegetables that didn't require mixing. "I'll be up right away to make bread," she said. "I don't think you'll run out before tomorrow."

We didn't run out of bread, but Ma was not up

the next day. Pa was worried. He stood at the window and watched the snow swirl around the porch. The barn was not visible from the house.

"I don't know how we'll get the doctor if this doesn't stop," he said. "We'll have to ask the Lord to take care of Ma until the storm is over."

"We could ask Him to tell the doctor to come," I suggested. "Then you wouldn't have to go after him."

"Yes," Pa said. "We could do that all right. God could certainly send the doctor here if that's His will."

That night, just as we were ready to go to bed, we were startled by a loud banging on the door. When Pa opened it, there, surrounded by snow and wind, stood the doctor!

"Thank the Lord!" Pa said as he pulled him into the kitchen. "We prayed that you would come!"

"What do you mean you prayed that I would come?" the doctor exclaimed. "You didn't even call for me! I was trying to get home from the Gibbs's place, and I was beginning to think I wouldn't make it anywhere when I saw your light."

"Anyway," Pa said, "the Lord sent you, and we're grateful."

The doctor took care of Ma and stayed until the following day. When the wind stopped blowing, the men and the boys were able to dig through the drifts. Soon everything was back to normal. That was certainly some storm; probably the worst I can remember. . . ."

"After that, I guess you believed your Pa could smell a storm, didn't you?" I asked.

"Yes." Grandma laughed. "We didn't doubt him again. But I lived many more years in the country, and I don't think I was ever good at sniffing out the weather."

I returned to the window to watch the snow and wish I could be snowbound, just once.

chapter seven

The Button Basket

Of all the things in Grandma's house that could delight a little girl, there was nothing that even approached the button basket. It sat high on the old china cabinet and was brought down on special occasions of confinement to bed, or possibly to soothe a severe case of disappointment. The basket looked rather ordinary from the floor. It was almost a foot in diameter and was tightly woven of dark brown reeds. But when one looked at the top, it was far from ordinary! Bright-colored beads were sewed in an unusual pattern. Some of the beads flopped when I ran my fingers over them, for the basket was old. Almost as old as Grandma, in fact.

"Where did you get the basket, Grandma?" I asked one day. "Did your mother buy it for you?"

"Oh, no," Grandma replied. "I should say not. That basket came in an unusual way."

Grandma looked fondly at the basket and continued her story. . . .

I WAS ONLY FIVE YEARS OLD WHEN it all happened, but I can remember very clearly that summer day. We lived in a new log house that Pa had just finished way up in the northern woods of Michigan. Our nearest neighbors were more than five miles away, and we seldom had company. Although the man from whom Pa bought the land had assured Pa that the Indians thereabouts were friendly, we still had a fear of meeting one of them, and never ran beyond the clearing without either Ma or Pa with us.

On this morning, Pa had left at dawn for the long drive into town for supplies. Ma had assured him that we would be all right alone. The boys were big (Reuben was eight and Roy was almost seven), and they would look after us women folks.

The day was fine and warm, and the boys had hurried through their chores and were playing a game with sticks and pine cones. I was swinging in the rope swing Pa had hung for me in the tree nearest the cabin. Ma was singing as she worked, and the boys were shouting, so it was not strange that no one heard when someone approached the cabin from the woods.

Suddenly, it seemed too quiet. The boys were

standing still and open-mouthed. Ma had stopped singing and was staring toward the woods beyond the clearing. For there, slowly and softly, came a tall Indian toward us.

"Children, come here," Ma called, and we quickly ran to hide behind her skirts.

"Now don't make any noise," she warned. "We don't want to scare him. Maybe he's lost or something."

She knew, or course, that he was not. Indians did not get lost in their own woods. She just needed to reassure herself as well as us.

The Indian was taller than anyone I had ever seen. Much taller than Pa. He wore buckskin trousers and had bright beads around his neck. His hair was in a long braid, and more beads were woven through the braid. He stood straight and broad-shouldered in front of Ma and held out his hand. Ma shrank back against the cabin, and I began to cry in terror.

It was Reuben who noticed that the Indian carried a brown basket. He held it toward Ma, as though wanting her to take it.

"It's a peace offering, Ma," said Reuben. "He wants you to have it."

Timidly, Ma reached out and took the basket. The Indian stood, watching her. Ma knew that she must give something in return, but what did she have? Quickly she turned and ran into the cabin and looked about frantically for something to offer the Indian.

"I'll get something shiny," she thought, and reached for the pewter cups she had brought from home. The Indian, however, shook his head. Ma offered him the only mirror we owned. He looked at it curiously, then handed it back with another shake of his head.

What did he want? How could she find out? The Indian stood in the doorway, his eyes taking in every detail of the little one-room cabin. Then he walked to the stove and uncovered the loaves of fresh bread that had just come from the oven. Food! Of course, that was it. As quickly as she could, Ma wrapped the loaves in a towel and thrust them at the Indian. We children watched wide-eyed as she added the remainder of our sugar supply, several cans of fruit, and the pie she had made for Pa's supper.

The Indian seemed pleased. He now held all he could possibly carry, and without a sound he turned and left the little cabin. We watched as he crossed the clearing with his bounty, and then Ma sank weakly to the doorstep as he disappeared quietly into the woods.

We did not venture away from the cabin again that day, and all of us were much relieved to see

Pa returning in the buggy as twilight fell. Everyone tried at one time to tell Pa what had happened. The basket was quite forgotten until Pa saw it lying on the bed where Ma had dropped it.

He picked it up and studied it carefully. "This is a beautiful piece of handiwork," he said. "It is hand-woven, and those beads would tell an Indian legend if we knew how to read them. I'd like to know the story."

"Well, I've had enough story for one day," replied Ma. "You can just put that basket away until I get my breath back and my heart is in place again."

"So the basket was put away. Eventually, however, Ma decided it would make a good sewing basket, so it was put to use. She insisted, however, that she didn't care enough about the story to want the Indian to come back and tell it to her!"

chapter eight

Little Gray Shoes

The winter I was six years old, I had diphtheria. After a few weeks, when I began to feel a little better, Grandma brought the basket to my bed. Most everything in Grandma's house had a story, but the basket was full of them!

The basket contained buttons . . . all sizes, shapes, colors, and kinds. There were so many things to do with them, that it was hard to know how to start. Should I sort out all the round buttons? Or string the red buttons all together? Or maybe see how many different shapes there were? I seemed never to get to the end of the possibilities.

On this day, as I dug to the bottom of the basket, my fingers felt a new shape—one I hadn't noticed before. I brought the button out and looked at it curiously. It was a small silver-grey triangle. It had no holes through it, nor a hook on the back. There seemed to be no way to sew it on anything.

"Grandma," I called. "Here's a button I never saw before. Where did it come from?"

Grandma came to look. She turned the button over in her hand thoughtfully.

"Why, this was one of my shoe buttons," she replied.

"Shoe button?" I asked. "Did you wear shoes with buttons on them? How was the button fastened on?"

"Oh, yes," said Grandma, "my shoes had buttons all the way up the side. The little hook that held this button came off long ago. I guess this is the only one that hasn't been lost."

Grandma continued to turn the button over in her hand. Her eye had the faraway look of a story, so I settled back on the pillows and waited. . . .

THESE WERE THE MOST BEAUTIFUL SHOES I had ever seen. We only had one new pair a year, and it was very important to make a good choice. Ma took me into town in September to shop for my new shoes. The first pair the man brought out were these wonderful gray shoes with silver triangle buttons. They were soft doe-skin, and to me, there had never been anything so lovely.

"Oh, Ma," I said. "These are the ones I want. I don't even want to look at any others."

"Well, try them on," said Ma. "We'll see."

The man put the shoes on my feet and buttoned them up with a tiny buttonhook. I held my feet straight out in front of me and admired those shoes. Oh, such beauty!

"Stand up," said Ma. "See if they are going to be too short."

Too short! Of course they weren't. They couldn't be. But when I stood down on the floor, my toes touched the end of the shoes.

"Do they pinch?" asked the man.

"Oh, no, they don't pinch! They are just fine!" I hastened to reassure them.

But Ma was doubtful.

"Remember," she said. "You have to wear these all year. It doesn't look like there is much room to grow. Do you have them in the next size?" she asked.

He didn't. All he had in the next size was a pair of black shoes with shiny patent leather toes and small round buttons. The thought of leaving those wonderful gray shoes was more than I could stand.

"These are just fine, Ma," I protested. "These fit just fine. They don't hurt a bit."

A little twinge told me that the shoes really were too small, and that I should tell Ma that my toes touched the end. But my desire to have a beautiful pair of shoes to show Sarah Jane and the other girls won out, and I said nothing.

Ma paid for the shoes, and they were wrapped for me to carry home in triumph. I wore them to church the following Sunday, and modestly accepted the admiration of my friends.

For a few weeks, the shoes only felt a little tight. Then as my feet continued to grow, they really began to pinch. Of course, I could say nothing to Ma. I could not admit that I had stretched the truth to get them, and anyway, there was no money to replace them. Finally I found that I could only wear the shoes when I was sitting down, so that I could curl my toes up inside. On Sunday morning, I would pull my boots on over my heavy stockings and carefully conceal my shoes under my cape until we got to church. Then I would sit through the long service with my poor feet aching in those beautiful shoes.

The day came, as I knew it would, when I could not get the shoes on at all. Ma had to be told. With much sobbing, I admitted that I had been deceitful about the shoes. Now it was only early in December, and I had no shoes to wear for the remainder of the winter.

Ma was sorry, not only that the shoes no longer fit, but that her little girl had deceived her. Oh, what I would have given for those homely black shoes that would fit! But that was impossible. There was no money for more shoes. The only solution was a pair of my older brother's outgrown shoes.

Pa tried his best to shine them up for me, but they were boy's shoes! And they had metal toes! I would never leave the house again. I would just stay home until it was time to go barefoot in the spring. But of course I didn't. Although I cried huge tears over them, I wore Roy's shoes to church. I did my best to hide my feet under the bench so no one would see, but such things are not easy to hide.

When Christmas came, I was delighted to see among my gifts a new rag doll that Ma had made and wrapped in a knitted shawl. But when I pulled back the shawl, what should look up at me but two gray shoe-button eyes! I looked quickly at Ma, but she acted as though nothing was wrong. I looked again at the doll. Her smiling mouth was not really laughing at me, I decided. In fact, she looked quite sympathetic. I touched the little buttons and thought how foolish I had been. This little doll would remind me to think twice before I did a deceitful thing like that again!

My gray-eyed Emily was my companion until I was too old for dolls. There were others, even one with a china head, but none so dear as Emily with her kind smile and shoe-button eyes.

Grandma dropped the button into the basket and went back to her work. I dozed off thinking of the gray shoes, and Grandma, a little girl just like me.

chapter nine

A Pig in a Poke

"Your surprise package came in the mail this morning," Grandma said to me as I came home for lunch.

"Oh, goody! Where is it?" I asked.

"Here on the table. Now don't be too disappointed if it isn't all you thought it would be."

I had ordered a "mystery box" from a magazine ad, imagining all sorts of lovely things that might be inside.

"I guess you had twenty-five cents worth of pleasure waiting for it," Grandma said when she saw the flimsy little toy the box contained.

"Next time I'll just spend my quarter at the store where I can see what I'm getting," I said. "I wouldn't have paid a nickel for this."

"That's what's called, 'buying a pig in a poke.' You aren't the first one to do that."

"A pig in a poke! What does that mean?"

"A poke is an old word that means a sack," Grandma

replied. "If you buy a pig in a poke, you pay for it without looking at it first; then you have to take what you get. It's not the smartest way to do business, but you may learn a lesson from it."

"Have you ever bought a pig in a poke, Grandma?"

"No, I didn't, but my brothers did. One of our neighbors sold his farm and was ready to move to another state. The day before he left, the boys went over to say good-bye. . . ."

THAT NIGHT AT THE SUPPER TABLE, Reuben asked Pa, "Could we use Nellie and the wagon in the morning? There's something we want to bring home from the Shaw's barn."

"What kind of something? We have several somethings in our own barn that could stand hauling off."

Reuben and Roy exchanged worried looks.

"Well," Reuben explained, "it's an old trunk. Mr. Shaw said we could have it, and whatever is in it, for just fifty cents."

"So, we put our money together and bought it," Roy added.

Pa put his fork down and looked at the boys. "Fifty cents! You mean you paid for the thing and didn't even look inside to see what you were getting?"

Reuben looked embarrassed. "We tried to," he mumbled, "but we couldn't get it open. Mr. Shaw said it hadn't been opened for fifty years or more, because no one could find the key."

"What in the world do you plan to do with a trunk full of who-knows-what that you can't even get into?" Pa asked. "Couldn't you think of a better way to spend your money?"

"It seemed like a good idea at the time," Reuben explained. "We thought we'd get it open some way, and it might be something really valuable."

"Very likely!" Pa snorted. "A trunk that has been sitting in the barn for fifty years is bound to be a real prize!"

"Can we take the wagon, then?" Reuben asked.

"Yes," Pa replied, "go ahead and take it. I hope for your sakes it's worth your time and effort."

The boys were sure it would be, and they spent the rest of the evening talking about the treasure they would have.

"If there's anything you like, we'll give it to you," Roy said to Ma. "There might even be a doll or something for Mabel."

"Thank you," Ma said. "That's generous of you. I just hope there's something in there you'll like."

Ma and I were at the window when the wagon pulled up the next morning, and we ran out to the porch. The boys looked delighted with themselves as they jumped down.

"Come and look, Ma," Roy called. "Can we bring it in the kitchen?"

"Mercy, no! You're not bringing fifty years of barn dirt into my kitchen. Put it up here on the porch."

"But what if it rains?" Roy said anxiously.

Ma eyed the rusty old hinges and scuffed-up leather. "One more good rain couldn't do anything but improve it."

So, groaning and puffing, the boys tugged it up the steps. It was about three feet long and a foot and a half high.

"If it's worth its weight in anything at all, you'll have a fortune," Ma said. "Did you hear a rattle in there?"

"No," Reuben replied. "It didn't move. It feels like one solid piece of iron to me."

"Part of the floor came up when we moved it," Roy put in. "I think Mr. Shaw's pa built the barn around it."

"Well, you boys can figure out how you're going to get it open while you're working today. Pa wants you to come help with the fence right away."

"Yes, ma'am," Reuben answered. "We'll work on it after dinner."

The boys went out to the field, and Ma and I went back to the kitchen.

"What do you think is in there, Ma?" I asked.

"I wouldn't have any idea. Usually folks keep things like quilts, or old photographs, or books, that sort of thing in them. I can't imagine what could be that heavy. I guess we'll have to wait until the boys get it open."

The rest of the morning I hung around the porch and watched the trunk. One time Ma called to me from the kitchen door. "Haven't you anything better to do than watch that piece of junk? You're not going to know one thing more than you do now until it's opened."

She pushed the door out with her foot and handed me a pan. "As long as you're sitting there, you can at least snap the beans for dinner. I know how you feel. I'm anxious to know what's in there, too."

The morning passed slowly, but finally Pa and the boys came in from the field. Reuben stopped at the barn and picked up a crowbar.

"Come and eat dinner first, boys," Ma said. "If I'm not mistaken, you'll need all the strength you can get to pry that open."

Ma wasn't mistaken. Try as they would, the boys were not able to open the trunk. Red-faced and breathless, they left to join Pa in the field.

"Oh, dear, we're never going to see what's in there," I said.

"I'm sure we will," Ma replied. "Pa will help them this evening. They'll find some way to open it."

I spent the afternoon dreaming about all the wonderful things the trunk might hold and hoping that some of them might come to me. When supper was over, Pa and the boys tackled the job again. The lid was rusted shut, and there seemed to be no place to get the crowbar under it. Finally, after much whacking and pounding, it began to look as though it might move.

"Let's give it another try," Pa said. They all leaned hard on the crowbar, and the lid cracked open. We crowded up close as Reuben pushed up the creaky top to reveal the contents.

"Nails?" he said.

Pa looked over Reuben's shoulder and nodded his head. "Nails!"

"Nails!" Roy yelped. "Is that whole trunk full of rusty old nails?"

It certainly looked that way. The nails were pitted and red and stuck together with rust. Reuben pushed his hand in as far as it would go and reported more of the same near the bottom.

"Seems to me I remember Bert Shaw saying that his father was a blacksmith before he bought the farm," Pa said. "This must be all that's left of the smithy. I don't know what you can do with them, boys. I don't think there's much call for rusty nails."

"That was an awful lot of work for something as useless as this," Reuben sighed.

"Besides, we lost fifty cents on it," Roy added.

"Seems to me there's something in the Bible about laying up treasures where moth and rust will not corrupt," Ma said. "Maybe this is a good example to remind us."

"I guess so," Reuben said. "But I'd just as soon someone else's fifty cents had paid for it."

"Let's haul the thing out to the barn. Maybe the peddler will buy them when he comes by again," Pa suggested.

The boys brightened up a little at that thought, and the trunk was moved to the barn. I don't remember whether the peddler took it or not, but I'm sure the boys didn't buy anything sight unseen again.

chapter ten

Nellie's Trips to Town

The rain was splashing down, and I was bored.

"Grandma," I said, "what did you do to have fun when you were a little girl?"

"Oh, my," said Grandma. "There was lots to do on the farm. We had a swing in the big tree. We played in the barn loft when it rained. We waded in the brook and picked berries. There was always something to keep us busy."

"Didn't you ever go away on any trips?" I asked. "Did you have to stay on the farm all the time?"

"We went to church on Sunday," said Grandma. "And sometimes we went to town with Ma and Pa for the day. That was a big treat."

Grandma worked on her crocheting a few moments. Then she chuckled and said, "I remember one trip to town that had a funny ending. Run and get me another ball of thread, and I'll tell you about it."

I hurried back with the thread, and Grandma began the story. . . .

IT WAS A FRIDAY, I REMEMBER. Pa had several errands in town, and Ma wanted to do some shopping. So it was decided that the whole family would go and make a day of it. The boys hurried through their chores while Ma and I packed a lunch to take along. We were soon ready and on our way.

I went with Ma to pick out dress goods and other things she needed, and the boys went with Pa. We were to meet at the buggy later in the afternoon to get our lunch. We were going to picnic in the little grove at the edge of town. Pa tied Nellie to a hitching post near the blacksmith's shop, and we all went our separate ways.

Ma and I took a long time picking out material and buttons and thread. Of course there were other things to look at, too. By the time we got back to the blacksmith shop, Pa and the boys were already there.

Pa was looking up the road with a puzzled expression, and the boys were running around the back of the shop. Nellie and the buggy were nowhere to be seen.

Ma wasted no time in coming to the point.

"Pa," she said, "where is Nellie?"

"I don't just know," Pa replied. "But she

doesn't appear to be here."

"Did you tie her tight?" Ma asked. "Could she have slipped the reins off the post and gone on home?"

"That's not likely," said Pa. "I'm sure I tied her as tight as usual. There must be some explanation for this."

"Well," said Ma. "I wish you'd find it in a hurry. Our lunch is in the buggy, and it's getting late."

"Yes, Pa," I said, "I'm hungry."

"We'll find Nellie, all right," said Pa. "Don't worry. I'll ask around and see if anyone saw her start away."

No one had. The blacksmith had noticed several buggies come and go, but he couldn't say who was in them. There were still several horses tied there, but none of them was Nellie. Anyone who had noticed a horse pulling an empty buggy would surely have stopped it.

Evening was coming on, and we children were getting hungrier, Ma was getting more worried, and Pa had exhausted all the possibilities he could think of. At last he suggested that we go to the minister's house to rest and decide what to do.

The minister's wife was surprised to see us, but very hospitable.

"Why, of course you'll stay here," she said, when she had heard the story. "And after supper,

Will can take you out to your place. I'm sure your horse must have gone on home."

We were glad she had mentioned supper. The thought of the long ride home with nothing to eat was not a pleasant one for us children. The women began to prepare the meal, and Pa and the minister discussed our problem. There was never any thought that Nellie had been stolen. People just did not steal horses and buggies in our little town. Perhaps some mischievous boys had untied the horse, but even that didn't seem likely with people around all the time.

There seemed to be no more to do about it that night, so after supper the minister hitched up his buggy, and we got in for our trip home. It was dark now, and only a few people were left on the street. Light shone from the blacksmith shop, however, and as we approached it, Roy called out, "Look, Pa! There's Nellie, right were we left her!"

The minster stopped the horse, and Pa jumped down. Sure enough, there was Nellie and the buggy. Pa walked around and looked at the horse in disbelief. Nellie looked back at him as if to say, "Well, where have you been? Don't you know it's dark?"

By this time, the rest of us were gathered around. The lunch still sat in the buggy, untouched. We were too astonished to speak.

Finally Pa said, "I guess we might as well go home. She's not going to tell us where she's been."

He thanked the minister for his help, and we climbed into our own buggy. The trip home was spent trying to find a reasonable explanation for what had happened. We could think of none. Pa was just glad to have the horse and buggy back and be on the way home.

Saturday morning we were still talking about the mystery when our neighbor, Ed Hobbs, drove into the yard. Pa went out to meet him, and invited him in to breakfast.

"Thanks," said Ed, "but I've already eaten. I just came to tell you folks what happened yesterday."

He sat down at the table and told us the story.

"I was pretty busy yesterday," he said, "and I had a broken plow that needed to be fixed. I couldn't spare my boy to take it into town, so Grandpa said he'd do it for me. Grandpa's getting pretty old, and doesn't see very well, but I thought he could probably make it to the blacksmith shop all right, so I loaded the plow in the buggy, and Grandpa started out.

"It wasn't until early evening, long after Grandpa had returned, that I noticed a strange horse in the barn. Then I saw the buggy out beside the shed. I went into the house to see who

76

was visiting. Grandpa was dozing by the fire, and there was no one else in the kitchen but the family.

" 'Grandpa,' I said, 'whose horse is that in the barn?'

" 'Why, it's our horse, naturally,' said Grandpa. 'Whose did you think it was?'

" 'That's not our horse, Grandpa,' I said. 'It looks like Brother O'Dell's horse and buggy to me.'

" 'Brother O'Dell?' said Grandpa. 'Is Brother O'Dell here? Why didn't he come in and sit a spell?'

" 'No, Grandpa,' I replied. 'Brother O'Dell isn't here. I think you brought his horse and buggy home.'

" 'Now why would I do a thing like that?' asked Grandpa indignantly. 'I wasn't anywhere near the O'Dells' place today!'

"I gave up on Grandpa," said Ed. "I hitched up your horse and drove it into town. There was our horse and buggy, right in front of the blacksmith shop. The blacksmith said you had been looking for your horse, but he didn't know where you had gone, so I tied her up and came on home. I figured I'd come and tell you about it first thing this morning. I'm sorry about Grandpa. I won't send him on any more errands into town!"

Pa laughed as hard as we children did. He assured Ed that everything had turned out all right, and Grandpa Hobbs was forgiven. We seldom made a trip to town after that but someone would say, "Remember when Grandpa Hobbs took Nellie home by mistake?" I guess that was the most memorable trip to town we had when I was a little girl.

Grandma continued to rock and crochet, and I returned to the window to watch the rain, and think what fun it would have been to be a little girl when Grandma was.

chapter eleven

Face Cream from
Godey's Lady's Book

Receiving mail always excited me. I never had to be told to get the mail for Grandma on my way home from school. But sometimes the mail became even more important. Like the time I was watching for something I had ordered from *Woman's Home Companion*.

When the small package finally arrived, my face revealed how excited I was.

"What did you get a sample of this time?" Grandma asked as I came in proudly carrying the precious box.

"You'll see. Just wait till I show you," I said, promising Grandma the box held something special.

Quickly I tore the wrapping paper off the small box. Inside was a jar of skin cream for wrinkles.

Grandma laughed when she saw it. "You certainly don't need that," she said. "Now it might do me some good if those things ever really worked."

"You aren't wrinkled, Grandma," I protested. "Your face is nice and smooth."

"Perhaps so. But not because of what I've rubbed on it. More than likely I've inherited a smooth skin."

She took the jar of cream and looked at the ingredients. "This doesn't look quite as dangerous as some stuff Sarah Jane and I mixed up one day. Did I ever tell you about that?"

"No, I'm sure you didn't," I replied. "Tell me now."

Grandma picked up her crocheting, and I settled back to listen to a story about Grandma and her friend, Sarah Jane, when they were my age. . . .

SARAH JANE HAD A COUSIN who lived in the city. This cousin often came to stay at Sarah Jane's for a few days. She brought things with her that we were not accustomed to seeing.

One morning as Sarah Jane and I were walking to school together Sarah Jane told me some very exciting news.

"My cousin Laura will be here tomorrow. She's going to stay all next week. Won't that be fun?"

"Yes," I agreed. "I'm glad she's coming. What do you think she'll bring this time?"

"Probably some pretty new dresses and hats," Sarah Jane guessed. "She might even let us try them on."

"Oh, I'm sure she wouldn't want us to try on her dresses. But maybe she wouldn't mind if we peeked at ourselves in the mirror to see how the hats looked."

Laura arrived the next day with several new hats. She amiably agreed that we might try them on.

They were too big, and had a tendency to slide down over our noses. But to us, they were the latest fashion.

As we laid the hats back on the bed, Sarah Jane spied something else that interested her. It was a magazine for ladies. We had not seen more than half a dozen magazines in our lives, so this was exciting.

"Oh, Laura," Sarah Jane cried, "may we look at your magazine? We'll be very careful."

"Why, yes. I'm not going to be reading it right away. Go ahead."

Eagerly we snatched the magazine and ran out to the porch. The cover pictured a lady with a very fashionable dress and hat, carrying a frilly parasol. The name of the magazine was *Godey's Lady's Book*.

"Ooh! Look at the ruffles on her dress!" Sarah Jane exclaimed. "Wouldn't you just love to have one dress with all those ribbons and things?"

"Yes, but there's little chance I'll ever have it," I replied. "Ma wouldn't iron that many ruffles for anything. Besides, we're not grown-up enough to have dresses like that. It looks like it might be organdy, doesn't it?"

"Mmm-hum," Sarah Jane agreed. "It looks like something soft, all right. And look at her hair. It must be long to make that big a roll around her head."

We spread the magazine across our laps and studied each page carefully. Nothing escaped our notice.

"I sure wish we were grown up," Sarah Jane sighed. "Think how much prettier we'd be."

"Yes, and how much more fun we could have. These ladies don't spend all their time going to school and doing chores. They just get all dressed up and sit around looking pretty."

We looked for a moment in silence; then Sarah Jane noticed something interesting. "Look here, Mabel. Here's something you can make to get rid of wrinkles on your face."

I looked where she was reading.

Guaranteed to remove wrinkles. Melt together a quantity of white wax and honey. When it becomes liquid, add the juice of several lemons. Spread the mixture liberally on your face and allow it to dry. In addition to smoothing out your wrinkles, this

*formula will leave your skin soft,
smooth, and freckle free.*

"But we don't have any wrinkles," I pointed
out.

"That doesn't matter," Sarah Jane replied. "If it
takes wrinkles away, it should keep us from
getting them, too. Besides," she added critically, "it
says it takes away freckles. And you have plenty
of those."

I rubbed my nose reflectively. "I sure do. Do
you suppose that stuff really would take them
off?"

"We can try it and see. I'll put some on if you
will. Where shall we mix it up?"

This would be a problem, since Sarah Jane's
mother was baking in her kitchen. It would be
better to work where we wouldn't have to answer
questions about what we were doing.

"Let's go to your house and see what your
mother is doing," Sarah Jane suggested.

We hurriedly returned the magazine to Laura's
bedroom and dashed back outdoors.

"Do you have all the things we need to put in
it?" Sarah Jane asked.

"I know we have wax left over from Ma's jelly
glasses. And I'm sure we have lemons. But I don't
know how much honey is left.

"I know where we can get some, though." I continued. "Remember that hollow tree in the woods? We found honey there last week."

Soon we were on our way to collect it in a small pail.

"This is sure going to be messy and sticky to put on our faces," I commented as we filled the pail.

"Probably the wax takes the sticky out," Sarah Jane replied. "Anyway, if it takes away your freckles and makes our skin smooth, it won't matter if it is a little gooey. I wonder how long we leave it on?"

"The directions said to let it dry," I reminded her. "I suppose the longer you leave it there, the more good it does. We'll have to take it off before we go in to supper, I guess."

"I guess so," Sarah Jane exclaimed. "I don't know what your brothers would say. But I'm not going to give Caleb a chance to make fun of me."

I knew what Reuben and Roy would say, too, and I was pretty sure I could predict what Ma would say. There seemed to be no reason to let them know about it.

Fortune was with us, for the kitchen was empty when we cautiously opened the back door. Ma heard us come in and called down from upstairs.

"Do you need something, Mabel?"

"No, Ma'am," I answered. "But we might like a cookie."

"Help yourself," Ma replied. "I'm too busy tearing rags to come down right now. You can pour yourselves some milk, too."

I assured her that we could. With a sigh of relief, we went to the pantry for a kettle in which to melt the wax and honey.

"This looks big enough," Sarah Jane said. "You start that getting hot, and I'll squeeze the lemons. Do you think two will be enough?"

"I guess two is 'several.' Maybe we can tell by the way it looks whether we need more or not."

"I don't see how," Sarah Jane argued. "We never saw any of this stuff before. But we'll start with two, anyway."

I placed the pan containing the wax and honey on the hottest part of the stove and pulled up a chair to sit on.

"Do you suppose I ought to stir it?" I inquired. "It doesn't look as though it's mixing very fast."

"Give it time," Sarah Jane advised. "Once the wax melts down, it will mix."

After a short time, the mixture began to bubble.

"There, see?" she said, stirring it with a spoon. "You can't tell which is wax and which is honey. I think it's time to put in the lemon juice." She picked up the juice, but I stopped her.

"You have to take the seeds out, first, silly. You don't want knobs all over your face, do you?"

"I guess you're right. That wouldn't look too good, would it?"

She dug the seeds out, and we carefully stirred the lemon juice into the pan.

"Umm, it smells good," I observed.

Sarah Jane agreed. "In fact, it smells a little like Ma's cough syrup. Do you want to taste it?'

"Sure, I'll take a little taste." I licked some off the spoon and smacked my lips. "It's fine," I reported. "If it tastes that good, it will certainly be safe to use. Let's take it to my room and try it."

We carefully lifted the kettle from the stove. Together we carried the kettle upstairs and set it on my dresser.

"It will have to cool a little before we put it on," I said.

"What if the wax gets hard again? We'll have to take it downstairs and heat it all over."

"It won't," I assured her. "The honey will keep it from getting too hard."

By the time the mixture was cool enough to use, it was thick and gooey—but still spreadable.

"Well, here goes," Sarah Jane said. She dipped a big blob out and spread it on her face. I did the

same. Soon our faces were covered with the sticky mess.

"Don't get it in your hair," I warned. "It looks like it would be awfully hard to get out. I wonder how long it will take to dry?"

"The magazine didn't say that. It would probably dry faster outside in the sun. But someone is sure to see us out there. We'd better stay here. . . . I wish we had brought the magazine to look at."

"We can look at the Sears catalog," I suggested. "Let's play like we're ordering things for our own house."

We sat down on the floor and spread the catalog out in front of us. After several minutes, Sarah Jane felt her face.

"I think it's dry, Mabel," she announced, hardly moving her lips. "It doesn't bend or anything."

I touched mine and discovered the same thing. The mask was solid and hard. It was impossible to move my mouth to speak, so my voice had a funny sound when I answered her. "So's mine. Maybe we'd better start taking it off now."

We ran to the mirror and looked at ourselves.

"We sure look funny." Sarah Jane laughed the best she could without moving her face. "How did the magazine say to get it off?"

Suddenly we looked at each other in dismay.

The magazine hadn't said anything about removing the mixture, only how to fix and spread it on.

"Well, we've done it again," I said. "How come everything we try works until we're ready to undo it? We'll just have to figure some way to get rid of it."

We certainly did try. We pushed the heavy masks that covered our faces. We pulled them, knocked on them, and tried to soak them off. They would not budge.

"I think we used too much wax and not enough honey," Sarah Jane puffed as she flopped back down on the bed.

"That's certainly a great thing to think of now," I answered crossly. "The only way to move wax is to melt it. And we certainly can't stick our faces in the fire!"

"Mine feels like it's already on fire. I don't think this stuff is good for your skin."

"You're going to have to think about more than that," I told her. "Or this stuff will be your skin. There has to be some way to get it off."

"We've tried everything we can think of. We'll just have to go down and let your Ma help us."

That was the last thing in the world I wanted to do. But I could see no other alternative. Slowly we trudged down to the kitchen.

Ma was working at the stove, and she said cheerfully, "Are you girls hungry again? It won't be long until suppertime, so you'd better not eat . . ."

She turned around as she spoke. When she spotted us standing in the doorway, her eyes widened in disbelief.

"What on earth . . .? What have you done to yourselves?"

I burst into tears. The sight of drops of tears running down that ridiculous mask must have been more than Ma could stand. Suddenly she began to laugh. She laughed until she had to sit down.

"It's not funny, Ma. We can't get it off! We'll have to wear it the rest of our lives!"

Ma controlled herself long enough to come over and feel my face. "What did you put in it?" she asked. "That will help me know how to take it off."

We told her.

"If you two ever live to grow up, it will only be the Lord's good mercy. The only thing we can do is apply something hot enough to melt the wax," Ma told us quickly.

"But we boiled the wax, Ma," I cried. "You can't boil our faces!"

"No, I won't try anything as drastic as that. I'll just use hot towels until it gets soft enough to pull away."

After several applications, we were finally able to start peeling the mixture off. As it came loose, our skin came with it.

"Ouch! That hurts," I cried.

But Ma could not stop. By the time the last bit of wax and honey were removed, our faces were fiery red and raw.

"What did we do wrong?" Sarah Jane wailed. "We made it just like the magazine said."

"You may have used the wrong quantities, or left it on too long," Ma said. "At any rate, I don't think you'll try it again."

"I know I won't," Sarah Jane moaned. "I'm going to tell Laura she should ignore that page in her magazine." She looked at me. "The stuff did one thing they said it would, Mabel. I don't see any freckles."

"There's no skin left, either," I retorted. "I'd rather have freckles than a face like this."

"Never mind." Ma tried to soothe us. "Your faces will be all right in a couple of days."

"A couple of days!" I howled. "We can't go to school looking like this!"

🁢

"We did, though." Grandma laughed as she finished the story. "After a while we were able to laugh with the others over our foolishness."

I looked at the little jar of cream that had come in the mail.

"I don't think I'll use this, Grandma. I guess I'll just let my face get wrinkled if it wants to!"

chapter twelve

High Society

I always thought of Grandma's folks as country people—warm and cheerful. The old home the family lived in for years was large. But I never thought of Grandma's family as rich.

Not until one day at school when I was describing the old farm home to my class.

"You must have had some pretty rich ancestors," my teacher commented.

As soon as I got home that day, I asked Grandma. "Were your folks wealthy?"

"Come to think of it, they were in some ways," Grandma answered. "But probably not the way your teacher meant."

"What other way is there? Rich means a lot of money, doesn't it?"

"Not always," Grandma replied. "Sometimes it means other things we hardly ever think of. I learned about some of them when I was your age."

I settled down at the table to hear Grandma's story as she sat crocheting. . . .

MA WAS BUSY MAKING BREAD when I came home from school one day. I could smell baked beans in the oven, and I knew we were having a favorite supper this evening.

"Mmm, that smells good, Ma. How long before we eat?"

"Oh, the usual time, I expect," Ma replied. "Sometime between the hour you're so hungry you can't stand it and the hour you starve to death."

I laughed at that, because it seemed as though we were always between those two hours. I watched Ma knead the bread. Her sleeves were rolled up above her elbows, and little wisps of hair were coming out around her face.

"We have a pretty hard life, don't we, Ma?"

She straighted up and looked at me with amazement. "Now why would you say a thing like that?"

"Well, Sarah Jane's cousin Laura is visiting from the city, and she says we do. Not just as O'Dells," I hastened to add. "But everyone who lives out here in the country. She says she doesn't know how we live without servants to do the work."

Ma went back to her kneading. "I can tell her if

she's really interested."

"That's what Sarah Jane's ma told her, too. But Laura says she thinks we must be terribly unhappy. Do you suppose we should be feeling bad, and we just don't know it?"

"That's a possibility," Ma admitted. "But I'd just as soon not find out." She deftly separated the dough and formed a panful of rolls. Then she set them on the back of the stove to rise. "I don't know what I'd do with a servant if I had one."

"She could do the cooking and baking."

"I'll take care of my own cooking and baking, thank you," Ma replied. "That way, I always know what I'm eating. Besides, I enjoy it."

"She could do the dishes. You don't always enjoy those."

"I have a perfectly good daughter who needs to know how to do dishes," Ma said. "How are you going to know how to run your own home when you grow up if you never help someone else do it?"

With a lot of servants, I thought to myself. But I wouldn't say that to Ma. I was convinced that she didn't know what she was missing.

As we sat around the supper table that night, my mind was still on the subject. "Pa, would you like to have a servant?"

"A what?"

"A servant. Someone to do your work for you."

"I don't mind having a hired hand at harvest time, but I don't want someone doing my work," Pa replied. "What would I do?"

Reuben was quick to offer some suggestions. "You could spend some time fishing, and some time just sitting around the house . . ."

"Not my house, you couldn't," Ma put in quickly. "I have enough to do without working around useless bodies. Now if you were old and feeble, I'd let you sit by the stove and chuck a piece of wood in now and then. But you're not, thank the Lord."

No one seemed to agree with me, so I didn't say anything more. I thought a lot about it, though, until an unusual happening straightened out my thinking.

A few days before school was out, Sarah Jane met me at the end of our lane. "Mabel! Have I got some news for you! You'll never believe it!"

"What? What is it?"

Sarah Jane was jumping up and down. "You just won't believe it!"

"Oh, for goodness sake, Sarah Jane. Are you going to tell me or not?"

"Of course I'm going to tell you! Just give me a chance. My cousin Laura has asked me to come to the city for a week as soon as school is out. She wants you to come, too. My ma is going to ask your folks tonight. What do you think of that?"

Sarah Jane was right. I didn't believe her. I had never been away from home that long in my life. The thought of visiting the city took my breath away.

"Do you think your folks will let you go?" Sarah Jane was saying.

"Oh, I hope so! I'll be good for the rest of my life if they will!"

"I don't think I'd mention that if I were you. Parents have a way of thinking you ought to be good without getting paid for it."

I nodded in agreement, and we walked on to school. All that day, I wondered if Ma and Pa would say yes. That evening when Sarah Jane's mother came over, I was sure the answer would be no.

But it wasn't! If Laura's parents really wanted two house guests, I could go. The next few days were a flurry of getting ready.

"I'll only need to take my very best summer dresses, Ma," I told her, "and my good shoes."

"What do you plan to wear to play in?" she asked me. "You can't run around outside in your good clothes."

"I don't think you run around outside in the city," I replied. "I think you just dress up and look pretty."

"That could get old in a hurry. You'd better

take a few things, just in case."

My box was packed and repacked several times before the Monday arrived to leave.

"If you don't stand still," Ma warned me that morning, "I won't have your hair combed by the time the Clarks get here. You don't want to keep them waiting, do you?"

I didn't, nor did I want to wait myself. So I stood as still as possible while Ma finished getting me ready. I couldn't eat any breakfast, but Ma insisted that I drink the hot cocoa.

Finally Sarah Jane and her folks arrived, and we were on our way to the city.

"Can you imagine having someone do everything for you?" I said to Sarah Jane. "We'll be real ladies, won't we?"

"Oh, yes. I don't think I'll ever want to come back home. I won't make a bed, or do a dish, or dust a chair all the time we're here. Laura's mama even has a seamstress to do her mending!"

"Her 'mama'?" I inquired.

"That's what Laura calls her. It's more stylish, you know. She calls her pa 'papa,' too."

I couldn't imagine acting stylish when I returned home, not with Roy and Reuben around. But I would remember how they lived in the city. Maybe, when I had a home of my own . . .

We arrived at our destination before dusk. As

we climbed down from the buggy, I regarded the big house with awe.

"It has three whole floors! Do they live on all of them?"

"Certainly," Sarah Jane assured me. "We'll sleep on the top one. There's a library and a music room, too, and a big yard to play in. I've never stayed here before, but I visited once with my folks."

We were ushered into a large hallway, and Laura came to meet us. "Oh, good," she exclaimed. "You're here in time for dinner. Come on in!"

I opened my mouth to say that we had eaten dinner at noon; then closed it again. Something told me that the less I said, the better off I'd be.

But when we were seated in a big dining room, lighted with gas lamps, I could no longer contain my curiosity.

"Where does Laura's mama fix her meals?" I whispered to Sarah Jane.

"She doesn't. The cook fixes them."

"But where?"

"In the kitchen, of course," Sarah Jane said. "It's downstairs."

"In the cellar?" I squeaked, and then blushed when everyone looked at me.

"It's not called the cellar," Sarah Jane explained. "It's the lower floor. We'll see it tomorrow."

We were taken to our room very early. Once we crawled into the strange bed, I lay for a long time looking at the ceiling.

"Sarah Jane," I said at last, "when do they eat supper here?"

"We just finished eating it a little while ago. Don't you remember?"

"But Laura called that dinner. At home we eat dinner at noon."

"Oh! Well, they call supper 'dinner,' and they call dinner 'luncheon,' " she explained. "You get the same stuff to eat, though."

That really didn't make good sense to me. But I decided if I were going to grow up to be a society lady, I'd better learn some of the finer points. I fell asleep thinking about eating in Ma's warm kitchen with the good smells of food cooking and wood burning.

The following morning as we watched Sarah Jane's folks drive off toward home, my heart sank. I almost wished I were going, too. The feeling only lasted a few moments, though, for Laura soon hurried us off to shop in the big stores.

"Don't lag behind me, girls," she warned, "or you'll get lost. You may never find the front door again."

"I think that might be the truth," Sarah Jane said. "We'd better keep an eye on her."

We didn't lose Laura. But we didn't see much that was in the store, either. She moved through the many aisles as if she were running a race. We were both glad to be back at the house, protected by the big spiked fence that surrounded it.

"This house doesn't really look very lived in, does it?" I asked as we sat on the steps.

"I guess it isn't, not as much as ours," Sarah Jane admitted. "Laura is out a lot, and her mama goes calling every day. Her papa works in a big office so he never comes home, except to eat at night and sleep."

"Why don't we go out to the barn?" I suggested. "Animals would remind us of home."

"That's not a barn," Sarah Jane sighed. "It's a carriage house. All it has is horses and buggies."

I was stunned. "No cows? No chickens? Where do they get their milk and eggs?"

"Buy 'em. They buy everything, or else have someone else make it for them. I always thought that would be sort of nice. But there's something nice about a big barn with cows bumping around in it."

I heartily agreed with her. Gloom settled over us as we thought about the days ahead.

We did have nice times, though. Laura and her folks did their best to make us happy. Nevertheless, when the Clarks' buggy came into sight at the end of our visit, both Sarah Jane and I were ready to start for home. I could hardly wait for the buggy to drive up our lane.

"Oh, Ma!" I cried when I finally burst into our kitchen. "Are you glad I'm back?"

Ma grabbed me and gave me a big hug. "I should say I am. It's been too quiet around here with no one helping me. Did you happen to bring a servant back with you?"

I shook my head. "We're not hard up at all, Ma. They don't have any food or milk or anything unless they buy it. We have it right here free! And they never get to eat in the kitchen, or sit by the cookstove, or walk in the woods. I'd rather be right here with you and Pa and the boys."

"Good," Ma said. "I was hoping you'd feel that way. People live all different kinds of lives. But this is where God has placed us, and I'm glad you're happy with it. You can tell us all about your visit at suppertime."

"Supper will really taste good tonight," I said as I started toward my room. "I haven't had one since I left home!"

chapter thirteen

The Haircut

One of the things I liked to do best when I was a little girl was to brush Grandma's hair. Sometimes just before bedtime, when she took her hair down for the night, I had the chance to do that. The big bone hairpins were carefully placed in the little china dish on her dresser, and all her beautiful, long hair would fall down her back.

"I never saw such long hair, Grandma," I said one evening. "Haven't you ever had it cut?"

Grandma handed me the brush and picked up her sewing. "You could almost say that," she laughed. "It was never all cut off short, but some of it did get cut once."

"Tell me about it," I begged. "How did it happen? Did you get in trouble for it?"

"I was in trouble, all right," Grandma replied. "But not so much for the cut hair as for what I did to cover it up."

Grandma thought for a moment, then began her story. . . .

田

IT WAS A DARK RAINY DAY. Sarah Jane and I were
playing in the upstairs rooms until the rain stopped,
and we could go outside. Sarah Jane had come
over early that morning to show me a birthday gift
she had received the day before. I was suitably
impressed, because I had never had anything that
nice. It was a beautiful, heart-shaped locket.

"What are you going to put in it?" I asked.
"You'll have to have something special for that
pretty locket."

Sarah Jane nodded. "I know. I'd like to have a
nice picture." She looked at me thoughtfully.
"You're my best friend. Do you have a picture I
could put in here?"

I shook my head. "I am afraid not. All the
pictures of me are in the big album downstairs. If
one was missing, Ma would notice right away."

Sarah Jane sighed. "It's a shame not to have
something to put in it." Then she brightened. "My
cousin has a piece of hair in her locket. You have
lots of curls. Maybe I could have one to put in
mine."

I was pleased that Sarah Jane wanted to put
something that belonged to me in her locket, but I
wasn't really sure about the hair.

"I don't know," I said. "I don't think Ma would

like it. I've never had my hair cut."

"She won't even see it," Sarah Jane insisted. "I'll cut it out from underneath."

"Well, be careful. I don't want to get into trouble."

I ran to get the scissors, then sat down on the footstool, and Sarah Jane went to work. She lifted up the top curls and chose one underneath to cut.

"This is a good one. All the others cover this spot. I'll only cut a little bit off the end, and you can see how it looks. Maybe you'd like some cut off every curl."

"Oh, I don't think so," I said quickly. "One will be enough. I'll be in trouble if Ma sees that much gone."

"Don't worry," Sarah Jane said. "I'm not going to hurt it."

She picked up the scissors and began to snip the end off the curl. Just at that moment, a door slammed downstairs and both of us jumped. The scissors closed on my hair, and three curls dropped to the floor!

"Oh! Look what you did! How am I ever going to cover up all those curls?"

"I couldn't help it," Sarah Jane said. "You shouldn't have jumped."

"Well, you jumped, too. How did I know you

had half my hair in your hand? You said just one curl!"

"The rest of them fell down in the way when you moved," she said. "I couldn't help it." I ran to the mirror and looked at my hair.

"Oh," I moaned, "wait until Ma sees that. I'm really going to get it this time."

Sarah Jane looked remorseful. "Maybe you can comb it some other way so it won't be noticed."

"Ma always combs my hair. There's no way to keep her from seeing it."

"You could put your sunbonnet on," Sarah Jane suggested. "That would cover it up."

"I guess I could," I said doubtfully. "Maybe I can think of some way to tell her before she sees it."

I ran to get my sunbonnet and tucked my hair up underneath it. No one would see what had happened until I had to take it off.

"Won't your Ma wonder why you're wearing a sunbonnet when it's raining?" Sarah Jane asked when I returned.

"You're the one who suggested it," I said crossly. "And you're the one who cut my hair off. Now you can just pray that the sun comes out."

Whether she did or not, I don't know; but very shortly the rain stopped, and the sun came out. We hurried as far away from the house as possible for the rest of the morning.

When dinner time approached, I had to think of some way to stay away from Ma.

"Sarah Jane, why don't you run up to the house and ask Ma if we can have some sandwiches for a picnic?"

"Oh, I can't," Sarah Jane said. "I promised Ma I'd be home by dinner time. I'll have to hurry now, or I'll be late. I'll try to come back this afternoon."

I sat on a rock and watched Sarah Jane run across the field. There was no need for her to rush back, I thought glumly. There probably wouldn't be anything left of me to visit.

I sat there as long as I dared. I knew Ma would send one of the boys to find me if I didn't come when the dinner bell rang the second time, so I trudged slowly toward the house, hoping against hope that Ma would be too busy to notice me. I arrived at the door just as everyone sat down at the table.

Ma glanced at me and said, "I thought you'd be gone home with Sarah Jane. Hurry and wash. We're ready to eat now."

I dawdled with the washing as long as possible, then slipped into my chair. Pa asked the blessing, and Ma began to dish up the food.

"Haven't you forgotten something, Mabel?" Pa asked.

"No, I don't think so, Pa."

"You've still got your bonnet on, silly," said Roy.

"Oh, that," I said quickly. "I'm going right back out after dinner. I thought I'd save time by not having to put it on again."

I bent my head over my plate and began to eat quickly. Since no one said anything, I ventured to look up. Everyone was looking at me in a strange way. Roy continued to stuff food into his mouth while keeping his eyes on me, but the others had stopped eating. I put my head down again.

"Mabel," said Ma, "is there something you ought to tell us?"

"Oh, no, Ma. It's just that Sarah Jane will be back after dinner, and we are doing something special down by the brook."

That would not have been the end of the matter, I am sure, except that at just that moment our neighbor, Mr. Hobbs, drove into the yard. Pa went out to meet him, and Ma hurried to set another place at the table. With a sigh of relief, I continued my dinner.

Mr. Hobbs came in and sat down, and after a few words with Pa about the crops, he said, "Well, Jim, do you have a young lady visiting you today?"

"This is just me, Mr. Hobbs," I said.

"Oh, so it is!" Mr. Hobbs exclaimed. "Why, with that fancy bonnet, I was sure it must be a fine lady from town."

Ma returned to the table with more food, and she looked at me with disgust. "Mabel, go take off that sunbonnet. You look ridiculous."

"I'm through eating now, Ma," I said. "Couldn't I please go outside?"

If Mr. Hobbs had not been there, Ma would have insisted that I obey her. But since he was, and I had finished my dinner, she allowed me to leave. Thankfully I ran back to the brook to wait for Sarah Jane. Finally she arrived, breathless, and dropped into the grass.

"What did your Ma say?" she asked.

"She doesn't know yet. I didn't take off my bonnet. I was just lucky Mr. Hobbs came." And I told Sarah Jane what had happened.

She sat up and looked at me in amazement. "Now you will be in for it. I've found that no matter how bad you are, you end up being twice as bad if you hide it from your folks. My Ma always says, 'Be sure your sin will find you out,' and it always does."

"Well, you're not much comfort," I retorted. "It's easy for you to say that, since it isn't your hair that's cut off."

"Take off your bonnet, and let's see it again,"

Sarah Jane said. "Maybe it doesn't look as bad as we thought it did."

I pulled off my sunbonnet, and Sarah Jane gazed at my tangled curls.

"It looks as bad as we thought it did," she said dismally. "I don't know how you're going to cover it up."

"It's a sure thing I can't go around wearing my sunbonnet until it grows out. I won't get away with that again. You'll have to think of something else."

"I will!" Sarah Jane cried. "It's your hair—" Then she stopped. "I guess you're right. It was my fault for wanting to put a curl in my locket. The only thing to do is go tell your Ma what happened, and let her punish me, too." She sighed. "When do you want to do it?"

"I won't have any fun sitting here thinking about it all afternoon," I replied glumly. "We might as well go now."

Slowly I replaced my bonnet, and Sarah Jane and I started for the house.

"What do you think she'll do?" Sarah Jane asked. "Will she spank us?"

I considered that for a moment. "No, I don't think so. Ma doesn't spank me very often, and she wouldn't ever spank you. It will be something worse than that. We probably won't be able to play together for a long time."

Ma was sitting on the porch, shelling peas for supper. As we approached, she looked up and smiled. "Did you girls have a nice time at the brook?" she asked. "I thought you'd be back up to the house before you went home, Sarah Jane. You forgot something."

Ma pulled Sarah Jane's locket and my curls from her apron pocket!

We gazed at them in silence. This was not at all what we had expected.

"I hope you've learned something today, girls," Ma said. "The hurting of your own uneasy conscience is worse than any punishment anyone else can give you."

She looked at my sunbonnet. "Covering something up doesn't make it go away. You knew I would see what had happened sooner or later, didn't you, Mabel?"

I nodded miserably.

"Well, come on," Ma said kindly. "Let's wash your hair and see if we can part it on the other side until that place grows out. I think you've suffered enough. We won't have to let Pa and the boys know what happened. . . ."

🔳

"And that's what we did," Grandma said. "Sarah

Jane and I never forgot that lesson. Fortunately, hair grows back again. Everything isn't that easily repaired, however."

"And did Sarah Jane get the curl for her locket?" I asked.

"Oh, yes," Grandma laughed. "Ma let her keep it. But she really didn't need it to remember me or that day."

chapter fourteen

Grandma's Day Off

"Would you set the table for me, please?" Grandma asked as she was getting dinner ready.

"I don't want to," I replied.

Grandma looked at me in surprise. "You what?"

"I don't want to," I said, a little less bravely this time.

"I don't believe I asked if you wanted to. I asked if you would."

While I placed the knives and forks around the table, I muttered, "Molly Stone never has to do anything she doesn't want to."

Grandma looked at me thoughtfully. "I'm not sure that's always true. Having 'stuff' to do makes you part of the family. You'd be unhappy if you never had to work."

I'd like to try it sometime, I thought.

Grandma seemed to have read my mind, for suddenly she laughed. "I wanted to try that once. I thought I was expected to do entirely too much around home, and that if I didn't have all my chores to do, I'd be perfectly happy."

"Did your mother let you try it?"

"Yes, she did," Grandma replied, "and I'll tell you how it turned out after dinner."

When we had finished the dishes, Grandma sat down with her sewing, and I pulled my chair up beside her. . . .

IT WAS IN THE SUMMER, the summer I was nine years old. Ma was very busy taking care of the garden, canning the early vegetables, and cooking for the hired men Pa had working on the farm. My job was to make the beds, help with the dishes, sweep the floors and dust, feed the chickens, and bring the cows in from the pasture in the evening.

Actually those chores didn't take a lot of time if I got right at them, but I grumbled and fussed until my work seemed to use up most of the day. One morning Ma became impatient with my complaining.

"You seem to forget that you're not the only one in the family who has work to do," she reminded me. "Pa and the boys aren't out in the fields playing ball, you know. Where would you be if no one in the family did any work for you?"

"I'd probably get along fine," I replied grumpily. "I could take care of myself if I didn't have all these other jobs to do."

Ma eyed me carefully for a moment. "All right. We'll try it and see. You finish up your work for today, and beginning tomorrow morning, you may do whatever you like. The rest of us will take over your chores."

"Do you really mean it, Ma?" I exclaimed. "I don't have to do anything except what I want to?"

"I mean it. But remember, no one will do anything for you, either. That will be your responsibility."

I couldn't believe my good fortune, to actually be free to spend my time in any way I chose. I began to plan all the things I would do in the glorious days ahead.

That night at supper, Pa regarded me thoughtfully. "I hear you're going to be a lady of independence."

"What does that mean, Pa?" I asked.

"It means that you are going to take care of yourself and be your own boss."

I nodded happily. "That's right. Ma said I could do whatever I want—and no chores to finish first!"

Roy opened his mouth to say something, but a look from Pa stopped him.

The following morning I awakened to the sound of voices in the kitchen. For a moment I wondered why Ma had not called me. Then I remembered—this was my day! I could sleep half the morning if I wanted to! Suddenly I didn't want to. The whole exciting day stretched before me, and I needed to get an early start.

I jumped out of bed and reached for my clothes. They were not there! The dress and apron I had taken off the night before lay on the floor where I had dropped them, but there were no clean things on the chair where Ma always placed them. I started to call her to come and help me, then decided against it. I could certainly get my own clothes out.

I dressed as quickly as I could and ran to the kitchen. To my surprise, the table was cleared, and Ma was doing the dishes.

"Where is my breakfast?" I asked.

Ma didn't turn around. "That's your responsibility. You go ahead and get what you want."

That slowed me down a little. I hadn't counted on having to fix my meals. I could see that the family had eaten pancakes and ham and eggs, but that was hard for me to fix, especially since the pancake batter seemed to be all gone. I finally managed to cut a piece of bread and put jam on it. The heavy milk pitcher was too much for me to handle. Milk spilled out on the table and floor.

"That's too bad," Ma said. "You know where the mop and bucket are, don't you?"

"Aren't you going to help me?"

"Why, no. You can take care of yourself."

When I had cleaned up the mess as best I could, I sat down at the table. A piece of bread and jam and no one to eat with seemed a poor way to start the day.

"I sure don't like to eat alone," I muttered.

"I'm sorry," Ma said. "But I thought since you had no chores today, you'd rather sleep in than get up when we did."

This reminder of the good times ahead brightened my outlook somewhat, so I finished quickly and hurried outside. The day was bright and beautiful, and I skipped happily across the yard. Immediately I was surrounded by chickens.

"Oh, bother! You'll just have to wait. Ma will feed you as soon as she has time."

It seemed to me that they watched reproachfully as I ran on toward the brook. *It won't hurt 'em to wait a few minutes,* I thought. *This is my day.*

For a while I was happy, picking flowers and wading in the brook. I made a daisy chain to hang around my neck, then lay on my stomach to see myself in the water.

After what seemed like a long time, I looked

up at the sun and saw that it was still only the
middle of the morning. Time didn't go so fast
when there was no one to play with. I thought of
Ma doing the dishes alone and making all the
beds, and began to feel a little bit guilty.

But after all, I thought, *she did say I could do
what I wanted to.* And that's what I was doing.

That morning went slower than any I had ever
known. I was determined not to miss the dinner
bell, so when it seemed close to noon, I started
back to the house. I wasn't late, but another
surprise awaited me.

The table was set for dinner, but at my place
there was nothing but bread crumbs and a knife
with jam on it!

Ma turned and smiled at me. "Did you have a
nice morning?"

"Yes, ma'am. But don't I get to eat with you
this noon?"

"Oh my, yes," Ma replied. "Just clear away
your breakfast things and set your place."

I did so, but my ideas about freedom were
beginning to change.

"Shall I help put the food on?" I asked.

Ma looked surprised. "No, thank you. Just sit
down, and we'll be ready to eat in a few minutes."

I sat down at the table and watched Ma dish
up the food. Something was just not right about

this arrangement, and it made me feel uneasy. But I decided not to let the boys know how disappointing it was. When they and Pa came in for dinner, I attempted to look happier than I felt.

"Well," Pa boomed as he sat down at the table. "Do we have a visitor here today?"

"I'm not a visitor, Pa," I said. "I live here!"

"Of course, how could I forget that?"

"I'd like to forget it sometimes," Roy added. "I could get along real well without her for a while."

I looked at Ma quickly, afraid that she might decide to send me away so Roy could try it out, but she was giving him a disapproving look, and he bowed his head for prayer. Pa prayed, as usual, for the Lord to bless the food and the hands that prepared it. It occurred to me that I hadn't helped, so the blessing was not for me.

"What are you planning to do with your afternoon?" Pa asked as he began to eat.

"I don't know exactly . . . but I'll have fun," I added quickly.

After dinner I wandered out to the porch and sat on the edge, swinging my feet. The rattle of dishes reminded me that mine would probably not be done unless I took care of it. When Ma finished and left the kitchen, I crept to the door to look. Sure enough, there was my cup and plate. The rest of the table was cleared.

That's not fair! I thought. *Ma did the boys' dishes. She could have done mine too.*

"And you could have helped her!" a little voice inside me said. "She did the boys' dishes, because they are out in the field working."

As quietly as I could, I rinsed off my dishes and brushed the crumbs from the table. I felt ashamed that I was the only one in the family who hadn't done anything all day. Even our dog, Pep, had taken the cows to the field that morning. Slowly I walked to my room to think things over. The unmade bed and the clothes on the floor looked worse than they had when I left them.

I picked up my clothes and made the bed, then sat down on the edge and looked around the room. Why had I thought that having no chores to do would be so wonderful? How had I planned to spend the time?

I picked up a mail order catalog and flipped over a few pages, then put it down. Emily sat in the chair watching me, her sober, shoe-button, doll eyes inviting me to play. But I didn't feel like it. The clock in the parlor struck. Only one hour had passed since dinner time!

I sighed and walked to the window. Ma was in the garden picking vegetables for supper. Maybe she would let me help her get them ready.

"Ma, I'm tired of being a lady of independence.

Could I shell the peas for you?"

"Are you sure you want to? What about your day off?"

"I think I've had enough of it. I can't think of anything I want to do."

"You've found out something important today!" Ma said. "It often happens that if you don't do anything, there's nothing you want to do. That's a pretty sad way to live."

I agreed with Ma, and I didn't try that again. . . .

Grandma looked at me, and her eyes twinkled. "Do you think you'd like to try it?"

I shook my head. "I don't think so. I guess it's nicer to have something to do."

chapter fifteen

Ma's Birthday Cake

Grandma was baking, and I had volunteered my services as onlooker and commentator.

"When can I bake something, Grandma?" I asked. "I'm old enough to bake by myself. I can read the recipe and measure things."

"Yes," said Grandma, "I believe you could. In fact, you would probably do a better job than I did the first time!"

Grandma laughed as she reached for the cookie pans. . . .

🏠

MA WAS GOING TO HAVE A BIRTHDAY, and I thought it would be a good idea to have a surprise party for her. I talked it over with Pa, and he agreed that it would be nice. We could have the party in the front yard. There were lots of trees and soft grass, and it would be an excellent place for all the neighbors to gather. How this could be accomplished without Ma suspecting, we didn't know, but we were determined to try.

Fortune was with us, for on the morning of the party Ma discovered that she had to make a trip to town before she could finish the shirts she was sewing for the boys.

"Mabel," she said, "how would you like to go into town with me this morning? We can leave right after breakfast and be back in time to get dinner for Pa and the boys."

Usually I would not have been able to finish my breakfast for thinking of a trip to town, but this morning my thoughts were on the party. What luck! With Ma gone, I could make her a birthday cake!

"I guess I won't go this morning, Ma," I replied. "I think I'd rather stay here."

Ma looked at me with concern.

"Are you sick?" she asked. "Do you have a fever?" She felt my head anxiously.

"Oh, no, Ma," I said quickly. "I feel just fine. I'll even do the dishes for you if you'd like to get started right away."

Ma looked puzzled, but she had no time to pursue the matter further.

I began to clear the table and get the dishes ready to wash. This was not usually one of my favorite jobs, but today was a special day. Ma was soon ready to leave. She stopped at the door and looked at me suspiciously.

"Are you sure you don't want to come?" she said. "Are you planning some kind of mischief while I'm gone?"

"Of course not, Ma," I said. "I'll be as good as can be. You don't have to worry about me."

Ma's look said that she would worry about me, but she got into the buggy, and I watched as she and Nellie disappeared down the lane. Quickly I finished the dishes and began to gather the things necessary for the cake. I knew exactly what was needed. I had watched Ma stir up a cake so many times that I hadn't the least doubt about my ability to make one too.

The oven would present a little problem. I decided to ask Pa to fix the fire for me, and I found him in the barn.

"Pa," I said, "I'm making a birthday cake for Ma. Would you build up the fire for me?"

Pa looked surprised.

"Are you sure you can do that by yourself, Mabel? You've never baked a cake before, have you?"

"No," I said, "but I've watched Ma a lot. I'm sure I can do it, Pa. Please let me try."

Pa was reluctant, but he came into the kitchen

and fixed the fire. After giving me careful instructions about the hot oven, he returned to the barn. I began happily mixing the cake in Ma's biggest mixing bowl. I had left out nothing, I was sure. The batter looked just wonderful.

As I greased the cake tins, I went back over the things I had put in the cake. Suddenly I remembered. The flavoring! I hadn't put any flavoring in it! Quickly I ran to the pantry and reached for the big Watkin's bottle that held the vanilla. Carefully I measured and stirred in the flavoring, and returned the bottle to the shelf.

The cake was ready to bake. I pulled my chair up near the oven to keep an eye on things. It was a warm spring day, and I longed to be outside, but I dared not leave my cake for a moment. What if one of the boys came in, slammed the door, and made it fall? Nothing must happen to ruin this cake.

Nothing did. It was high and golden brown. It looked every bit as good as Ma's cakes. Proudly I set the tins on the table to cool. I only had to make the frosting and hide the cake before Ma returned.

When the buggy turned in the lane shortly before dinner time, I was swinging under the big tree. I ran to help Ma with her bundles as Roy led Nellie to the barn. I longed to tell her my secret,

126

but of course I couldn't. This was to be a surprise party!

If Ma suspected anything, she didn't let on. She returned to her sewing, and I spent the afternoon hanging on the front gate, waiting for the first arrivals to the party. They were to come at supper-time, and the ladies would all bring something good to eat. I was sure that no one would come with as beautiful a cake as mine, though.

And I was right. Ma was surprised and pleased.

"You made this all by yourself, Mabel?" she asked. "Why it is just lovely. I had no idea you could do that alone!"

Proudly I handed Ma the knife.

"You must have the first piece, because it's your birthday," I said.

Ma cut the cake, and took a large slice on her plate. She took a bite, and an odd look came over her face. Something was wrong, I thought. But what could it be? I watched anxiously, but Ma kept on eating. Satisfied with my success, I ran to play with the other children.

That evening, when the last guest was gone, we sat in the kitchen talking over the surprise.

"And the biggest surprise was Mabel's cake," Ma said. "It was the most unusual cake I've ever eaten. What did you use to flavor it, Mabel?" she asked.

"Why the vanilla, Ma," I said. "Just like you always use."

"Show me where you got it," said Ma. "Where did you find the vanilla?"

Ma followed me to the pantry, and I pointed to the big bottle on the shelf. Ma took it down and looked at it, then she began to laugh. On the front of the bottle the label read, WATKIN'S LINIMENT.

Ma wiped her eyes and hugged me close.

"That's all right, Mabel," she said. "It was a lovely cake. A little liniment never hurt anyone. I couldn't have asked for a better birthday present."

Grandma put the cookies in the oven and began clearing the table. She looked thoughtfully at the Watkin's vanilla bottle.

"Those bottles do look a lot alike," she said. "I'm surprised I haven't done the same thing again. But no one except Ma would have been brave enough to eat it if I had!"

"I would, Grandma," I assured her. "I'd eat anything you made."

And I would, too. Even now, if I had the chance.

129

chapter sixteen

The Autograph

"Mabel, a package came in the mail for you today," Ma told me as I came in from school.

"For me? What is it? Who sent it?"

"How about opening it up to see?" Ma suggested.

Eagerly I tore open the wrappings and discovered a small, leather-bound volume. As I picked it up, a letter dropped out.

Dear Mabel,

I have come into possession of a copy of John Greenleaf Whittier's poem, "Snowbound." In remembrance of a similar occasion we shared, I would like you to have it. It is an autographed copy, since Mr. Whittier is a friend of my Quaker cousin, Eben White.

Yours truly,
Cousin Agatha

"Oh, Ma!" I cried. "Look at this! A book all my own! And signed by the author!"

"What a nice thing for Cousin Agatha to do," Ma said. "You must take good care of this."

"Oh, I will," I promised. "I can't wait to show it to Miss Gibson and the others. Maybe she'll read it to the school."

"Are you sure you should take it to school?" Ma asked doubtfully. "It's a pretty valuable gift."

"It will be safe," I assured her. "I won't let it out of my sight. I can't wait to see Warren's face when I show him. He thinks Whittier is the best author in our reader."

Sarah Jane was impressed when I showed the book to her.

"That's really nice," she said. "Your Cousin Agatha must think a lot of you to send something like that."

I nodded. "I think a lot of her, too. After we really got to know each other, she turned out to be a nice old lady."

"But do you think it's safe to take it to school?" she asked.

"You and Ma are just alike!" I exclaimed. "Why wouldn't it be safe? Do you think I'll lose it between here and there?"

"It wouldn't be the first thing you'd lost between here and there," Sarah Jane snickered. "I couldn't begin to recall all the stuff that has disappeared while you were looking the other way."

"Oh, for goodness' sake," I sniffed. "This book is not going to disappear. Give me credit for some sense."

"I was just teasing, Mabel. I'm sure you'll take good care of it."

As I expected, Miss Gibson was delighted with the book. "This is something you will always treasure, Mabel," she said. "An autographed book is a special thing to have."

I had guessed that Warren would be envious of my good fortune, but I wasn't prepared for his reaction. He looked carefully through the book and studied the name written on the flyleaf.

"What will you take for this, Mabel?" he asked me.

"Take for it! What do you mean?"

"I want it," he said. "I'll give you whatever you ask."

For a moment I was speechless, but Sarah Jane wasn't.

"You mean you'd pay Mabel for that book?" she asked.

Warren nodded. "As much as five dollars. That's all I have saved."

"You would pay five dollars for this book?" I

gasped. That was more money than I had ever had in my life. "You can buy a copy in town for twenty-five cents!"

"Maybe so," Warren said. "But I couldn't buy the autograph. That's what makes it valuable."

I looked at my book with even greater appreciation and shook my head. "I can't sell it, Warren," I said. "It was a gift. I don't have very many books that aren't schoolbooks, either."

"You could afford to buy quite a few with what I'd give you," he replied. "But you think it over and let me know if you change your mind."

"I'm sure I won't," I said to Sarah Jane as we left school together. "I can't imagine anything that I'd give up my book for."

"I'll say one thing for you, Mabel—you're not greedy," Sarah Jane observed. "Some people would sell their own brother to get five dollars."

"Don't think I haven't considered it," I said. "I just haven't had a whole lot of offers for Roy."

A few evenings later I found Pa sitting at the kitchen table, looking at a mail-order catalog.

"What are you looking for, Pa?" I asked. "Are you shopping for Christmas already?"

"Not exactly," Pa answered. "But I am thinking about winter. Your ma needs a new coat badly, and I'm trying to figure how we can get one for her after the crops are in. If we have a good yield,

I might be able to afford this one." He pointed to a neat cloth coat that came in gray, navy blue, or black.

"Oh, but look Pa. Here's one with a fur collar. Wouldn't that be warm and pretty?"

Pa looked at it wistfully. "Yes, it surely would. It would also cost about five dollars more than I can pay."

Five dollars! If I sold the book to Warren, we could get that coat for Ma. Excitedly I told Pa of the offer, but he shook his head.

"I can't let you do that, Mabel. Ma wouldn't hear of it if she knew. It's a very loving thought, though, and I thank you."

I said no more to Pa, but I thought about it a lot. Since the book was mine, I could sell it if I wanted to. And I did want Ma to have that lovely coat. Certainly after it was done and I had the money, Pa wouldn't object. I went to bed that Friday evening with the determination that I would tell Warren of my decision on Monday morning.

Before I blew out the light I looked through the book again and studied the delicate writing in the front. What a beautiful name—John Greenleaf Whittier. I sighed and put the book back. It was nice to have owned it for a little while, anyway.

On Saturday, as was our custom, Sarah Jane

and I went to town. We spent the usual amount of time looking through the general store and surveying the new things that had come in during the week. I told Sarah Jane of my plan.

"I guess you're doing the right thing," she agreed reluctantly. "Our folks give up a lot of things for us. Maybe we should try to pay them back more often."

We had just about finished browsing through the shelves and counters when Sarah Jane spied something.

"Mabel, look!" she cried. "Here's a copy of 'Snowbound' like yours. And it's just like you said—only twenty-five cents!"

I turned the book over in my hand. "It's just like Warren said, too. It's not autographed."

"I don't think the one in your book would be too hard to copy," Sarah Jane said slowly. "I believe I could do it so you'd never know the difference."

"Sarah Jane! Are you serious?"

"Of course I am," she replied. "You'll have your book and the five dollars, and Warren will have his autographed copy of 'Snowbound.' "

"But that's forgery!" I cried. "It's against the law."

"Oh, for goodness' sake," Sarah Jane replied. "I'm not going to cash it at the bank. It certainly won't defraud Mr. Whittier. You can write whatever you want to in your own books. Are you going to buy it, or not?"

I bought the book, and we hurried home with it. I had a nagging feeling that what we had planned was wrong, but I did want the money— and the book.

Sarah Jane practiced on a piece of paper until we both agreed that the signature looked just like the one Mr. Whittier had written.

"Now I'm ready to put it on the flyleaf," Sarah Jane decided. "Go sit on the bed or somewhere so you won't jab my arm. As nervous as you are, you'd probably tip the ink bottle over."

I sat across the room while she painstakingly copied John Greenleaf Whittier on the front page of the new book. When she had finished, she sat back and admired it.

"You'll have to keep these separated," she declared. "You'll never be able to tell which is the original."

I went to look, and I had to agree she was right. As far as I could tell, the signatures were identical.

"It's beautiful," I said, "but somehow I don't feel right about it. Warren will think he's paying for the real thing."

"He's paying for an autographed copy," Sarah

Jane said. "That's what this is. If you have to be so fussy, show him both books and let him take his pick. If he chose the wrong one, it wouldn't be your fault. You'd at least have a fifty-fifty chance of keeping yours."

I didn't chatter as I usually did while I helped Ma get supper, and she looked at me anxiously. "You're awfully quiet tonight, Mabel," she said. "Is something the matter?"

I shook my head. "No, I guess not. Ma, would it be wrong to sign someone else's name to something?"

"It depends on the reason for signing it," Ma replied. "If it was intended to deceive, then that's wrong. Under ordinary circumstances I'd say it's probably not a good idea. Are you planning on signing something?"

"Oh, no," I said. "I just wondered."

I didn't sleep well that night. I dreamed that I was caught in a snowstorm and Warren wouldn't help me because I had cheated him. I woke up to find my comforter on the floor and my heart pounding. Since I couldn't go back to sleep, I thought about going to church the next morning and trying to worship God. I knew I couldn't do it—not with the guilty feeling I had.

I soon discovered that I wasn't alone. Sarah Jane appeared right after breakfast.

"Mabel, you're right. We can't deceive Warren like that. I had terrible nightmares all night about what I did. I told the Lord I was sorry, and now I'm telling you. I feel bad about your money, but I don't think it's worth sinning for five dollars."

"It's not worth it for any amount," I told her. "I'd already decided that I would give Warren the real one. I don't want to remember any dirty tricks every time I look at Ma's beautiful coat!"

"Right!" Sarah Jane laughed. "And you said yourself that you couldn't tell the difference. I'll add my name down in the corner, and you'll have a real treasure to keep!"

Grandma's Prayer

The day was very hot, and I flopped down on the steps where Grandma was shelling peas for supper.

"Oh, dear," I complained, "why does it have to be so hot? Couldn't we pray that the Lord would send us some cold weather?"

Grandma laughed and threw me a pod to chew on.

"It will be cooler when the sun goes down," she said. "I don't think the Lord wants us to pray for something like that. In fact, I learned that lesson the hard way."

The heat suddenly seemed a little easier to bear if there was to be a story, so I settled back on the step and waited expectantly. Grandma smiled to herself and began. . . .

IT HAPPENED THE SUMMER I was nine years old. It was a day in August, much like this one. Pa had been up to the house several times for a cool drink, and finally said to Ma, "I guess I'll have to give up on the fences until later. It's just too hot to work out there. But if this heat doesn't let up so I can finish, we won't be able to get in to town on Saturday. I'll have to work early in the morning and after the sun goes down."

Pa returned to the barn, and I sat beside the cellar door thinking about what I had heard. Not go to town on Saturday! That just couldn't be! Sarah Jane and I had planned the whole day, and I just couldn't miss it.

I turned the problem over in my mind for some time. What could I do about the heat? Nothing, of course. And if Pa said no trip, then it was no trip.

After supper, Pa took down the big Bible for prayers. The Scripture he chose perked me up considerably. He read, "If you ask anything in my name, I will do it."

That was the answer! I'd pray for cool weather tomorrow so that Pa could finish his fences. While Pa thanked the Lord for His goodness to us and asked His blessing on our home, I had just one request: "Please make it cool tomorrow."

I awoke early the next morning, and ran to the window to look for clouds. I knew at once that my prayer was not answered. The sun was coming up, and the sky was clear. It promised to be as hot as yesterday, or perhaps even hotter.

I ate breakfast in glum silence. Maybe I hadn't prayed hard enough. Or maybe I didn't promise enough in return. As soon as I had finished helping Ma in the kitchen, I hurried to my room to ask the Lord again for cool weather. This time I promised to be obedient, kind to my brothers, and more help to Ma.

I was so sure I had been heard that it was no surprise to hear Ma say, shortly after noon, "Would you look at those black clouds coming over! Mabel, run and shut the windows in the boys' room. I believe it's going to rain!"

The sky grew blacker and a chill breeze came around the porch as I watched the results of my prayers. To tell the truth, I was becoming a bit worried. This didn't look like an ordinary rain storm to me. And it wasn't. In a few minutes, the clouds broke and it began to hail. Pep ran yipping under the porch, and I hurried inside to be nearer to Ma.

The storm was over in a short time. Pa and the boys came in from the barn, and Pa dropped heavily into a chair.

"Well, Maryanne," he said, "that did a lot of damage to the wheat. We may be able to save some of it, but it was pretty badly beaten."

I didn't listen further. I ran to my room and threw myself on my bed. The wheat was ruined, and it was all my fault. What would Pa do to me when he found out? I had just prayed for cool weather, not total destruction! Probably I had promised too much this time. What would the family think of me if they knew I had brought on this terrible hail storm? I was determined that they should not find out.

But when Pa prayed that evening, and thanked the Lord for His blessing and care, I couldn't stand it any longer. I began to sob and cry, and Ma looked around in concern. Pa picked me up and put me on his lap, and finally the story came out.

"Why, Mabel," said Pa, "don't you worry about that. Just remember that the Lord doesn't expect us to ask favors for our convenience or pleasure. A hail storm often follows a hot spell like this, and your prayers didn't bring it on."

Grandma picked up the pans to carry them to the kitchen.

"I was comforted by Pa's assurance," she said. "But I didn't forget that day. It taught me to pray for the Lord's will instead of demanding what I wanted."

chapter eighteen

The Seamstress

"Ma, did you remember that we're having an ice-cream social at school in two weeks?"

"Yes," Ma replied. "I remember. And I'll have a cake ready for you to take; don't worry about it."

"It's not the cake I was thinking about," I told her. "It just came to me that a new dress would be nice."

Ma looked up from the bread she was kneading. "It would be fine, but I have more projects going now than I can finish in two weeks. Your good dress looks all right."

"How about letting me make it myself?" I ventured. "I'm sure I could do it. I've watched you sew all my life."

"I've watched Pa mend harnesses, too, but I'm not going to try it," Ma retorted. "There's more to making a dress than sewing a seam. It's always nice if it fits when you're finished."

"I can't learn any younger," I said. "At least that's what you and Pa say when you want me to do something."

"You win, Mabel," Ma laughed. "I'll get the patterns out after dinner and see if I have something easy to start on."

As soon as the dishes were cleared away, Ma brought her pattern box to the table.

"Here, I like this," I said.

"I don't think you should try pleats," she protested. "You don't want anything with little tucks, either. They're awfully hard to make even."

"How about gathers? I could do that, couldn't I?"

Ma looked doubtful, but after going over all the patterns, she sighed. "That seems to be our only choice. I guess there's not a whole lot you could do wrong to a gathered skirt."

Sarah Jane was skeptical when I told her that I was making my dress for the ice-cream social.

"You don't have enough patience, Mabel. You know how you hate to take things out and do them over. You'll get tired of that the first day."

"What makes you think I'll have to take anything out?" I protested. "I just could have it right the first time, you know."

"I suppose you could," Sarah Jane conceded. "But you'll have to admit it isn't very likely."

She was right, of course. I had a habit of doing

things in a hurry and then finding mistakes.

Ma was concerned about that, too.

"Let me check each step before you go on to the next, Mabel," she said. "If you have to take something out, it will be easier before the whole dress is put together."

"No one has any confidence in me," I grumbled. "Why do you all assume I'll get things wrong?"

"We have nothing but past experience to go on," Ma replied. "But don't be discouraged. We learn by our mistakes."

"If I'd learned from every mistake I've made, I'd be twice as intelligent as I am."

Ma laughed and went back to her work. Later, when the dress was cut out, I began by putting the skirt together. Straight seams were not difficult, and when I showed them to Ma, she nodded.

"That's fine. Now pin the bodice together and baste it. We'll see if it needs tucks anywhere."

"Pin, baste, and sew," I muttered. "You don't do all that when you make a dress."

"Neither will you when you've put several hundred of them together," Ma replied. "Believe me, you'll save time in the long run."

The top of the dress was more complicated. After I had pinned the two sections of the back to the front, an extra long piece of material hung at the bottom.

"These parts don't match," I called to Ma. "You must have cut them wrong."

She came to look. "They aren't cut wrong. You didn't put the darts in the front."

I unpinned the pieces and placed the darts where they belonged.

"Aren't you glad you didn't just sew those together?" Ma asked me. "Pins are easier to remove than stitches."

Ma was right, but I was in no mood to agree. I was already tired of the dress.

Finally I had the bodice basted together, and I put it on for Ma to check. But when I went to find her, she had gone out to work in the garden.

"I can't go out there in nothing but my underskirt and a dress top," I grumbled to myself. "And who knows how long before she'll be back?"

I went back to Ma's bedroom to look in the mirror. The dress certainly looked perfect to me. Why waste time when it was all ready to sew? Ma might be out there for another half hour. I'll just go ahead and sew it up, I decided, and surprise her.

Sarah Jane appeared at the door just as I finished the last seam.

"I thought I'd come and see how you're doing on your dress," she said. "Is it all done?"

"Don't be silly," I replied. "I've just started. But I do have the sides of the skirt sewed up, and I just finished putting the top together." I whipped it off the sewing machine and held it up for Sarah Jane to see. "Doesn't it look nice?"

There was a silence as she took the piece and stared at it oddly.

"Mmm. But, Mabel, aren't you supposed to sew the seams on the wrong side of the material?"

"What do you mean?" I gasped, snatching it back. "Oh, no! I didn't turn it wrong side out before I basted it, and I sewed over the basting! What will I do now?"

"You know how much I hate to say 'I told you so,' " Sarah Jane snickered, "but my guess is that you'll take it out."

I rushed to the window and looked toward the garden where Ma still worked. "I can't get all those stitches picked out before Ma comes in," I said. "She'll say more than 'I told you so'! I was supposed to let her look at it before I sewed."

"Don't stand there moaning," Sarah Jane said. "Start working on it. You'll never get it taken apart by having hysterics."

Suddenly I spotted Ma's scissors on the table. "I'll cut them off," I declared.

"You'll do what?"

"I'll cut the seams off. Then I can turn it wrong side out and start over. That way she'll never need to know."

"In all the years I've known you, you've never been able to keep anything from your ma," Sarah Jane told me. "You were just not meant to be deceitful. Or your ma wasn't meant to be deceived."

I was already cutting away the seams.

"This isn't deceit," I replied. "This is survival. I'm learning how to turn my mistakes into intelligence. Put these scraps in the stove, will you?"

I turned the pieces wrong side out and was pinning them together when Ma came in.

"My goodness," she exclaimed. "Is that as far as you've gotten? Seems to me you were doing that when I went outside."

"I don't think I should hurry, do you, Ma?" I said. "I want it to look real nice."

Sarah Jane choked and hurried over to the water dipper.

"I guess I'd better go, Mabel. You've got a big job there, and I wouldn't want to disturb you." She rushed out the door, leaving Ma looking after her in surprise.

"She didn't stay very long, did she?"

"She stayed long enough," I told Ma. "And she'll be back. You can count on that."

I sat down with a sigh and prepared to baste the pieces together again. This time I'd let Ma see it before I stitched it on the machine.

"All right, Ma," I said finally. "Is it ready to sew?"

Ma looked critically at the front. "Something doesn't look right," she said with a frown. "Come here and let me see the back."

I went over to her and turned around.

"Why, what in the world!" she exclaimed. "It doesn't come together in the back! Did I cut it too small?" She took it off me and turned it wrong side out. "How wide did you make the seams?" She sat down and looked at it in bewilderment. "I can't believe I could have done that. And here I was talking about your mistakes."

Ma was so dismayed that I couldn't stand it. I threw my arms around her neck and cried.

"You didn't do it, Ma," I sobbed. "I did." And I told her what had happened. She put her head down on the table, and her shoulders shook with laughter.

"I don't see what's funny," I sniffed. "I can't wear a dress that doesn't meet in the back."

Ma wiped her eyes and picked up the bodice. "I suppose we could piece it," she suggested.

"Piece it!" I howled. "I won't appear at the ice-cream social in a dress that's pieced together like a quilt!"

Ma began to laugh again. "That's all the material I have like that, Mabel, or I'd cut out another bodice for you. Maybe I can salvage enough for an apron." She rolled up the skirt and top and handed them to me. "Put these in my room, please, and set the table for dinner."

I could hear her chuckling as she washed and cut up the vegetables. Somehow I felt worse than if she'd scolded me.

"I know what you mean," Sarah Jane said when I told her the story the next day. "If you get scolded, you know you deserved it. But if you get laughed at, you just feel stupid."

We walked a little way in silence. Then Sarah Jane began to giggle. "Your ma's not going to let you make the apron, is she?"

I glared at her.

"I was just going to suggest that if she did, the material would make nice carpet rags when you've finished with it."

Sarah Jane ducked and ran up the lane ahead of me.

"You'd better run," I hollered, "or I'll make a carpet rag out of you!"

chapter nineteen

What Grandma Lost

"I am going to wash some of your sweaters," Grandma said. "If you'll get your mittens, I'll wash them, too."

"I can't find them, Grandma," I told her.

"Haven't you looked for them?" Grandma asked. "You wore them to school today, didn't you?"

"No, I haven't had them for a couple of days," I replied. "I don't know where I left them."

"Now that was a careless thing to do," Grandma scolded. "It seems as though you could put your mittens in your pocket where they'd be safe."

Then she laughed.

"I guess I shouldn't scold you about mittens," she said. "I lost something a lot bigger than that when I was your age."

Of course I was anxious to hear about it, so when Grandma had finished the sweaters, she sat down with her sewing and began the story. . . .

IT WAS IN THE SPRING, I REMEMBER. It was an unusual day, because both Reuben and Roy were sick. Ma was quite concerned about them, and she hadn't paid much attention to me that morning. It wasn't until I was ready to go out the door that she really noticed me.

"Where are you going, Mabel?" she asked.

"Why, I'm going to school," I replied. "It's time to leave."

"Oh, no, Mabel," Ma said. "You can't go by yourself. You've never walked all that way without one of the boys. You'll just have to stay home today too."

"Oh, Ma!" I cried. "I don't want to stay home! I feel just fine. I can take Nellie and the buggy; then I won't be alone."

Ma looked doubtful, but she had the boys on her mind, so she said, "Well, go ask Pa about it. If he says it's all right, I suppose you can."

I hurried out to the barn, sure that Pa would see things my way. But he was reluctant, too.

"I'd take you to school myself, Mabel," he said. "But with both boys sick, I'm behind in the chores this morning. I'm not sure you can handle Nellie."

"Oh, Pa," I said. "You know I can. I've even

driven her to town when you were along. She knows the way to school, even if I don't show her."

Pa regarded me thoughtfully for a moment.

"I guess you can't start any younger," he said. "Just be careful and don't try any fancy tricks."

"Oh, I won't, Pa," I assured him. "I'll be extra careful."

I ran back to the house to tell Ma that I could go, and Pa hitched Nellie to the buggy.

I felt pretty proud, I can tell you. I didn't know of another girl at school who was allowed to bring a horse and buggy by herself. A lot of the boys did, of course. In fact, some of them just rode their horses to school.

As Nellie clip-clopped along the road, I began to imagine what the boys would think if I should come riding up to the school house on my horse. They would certainly take notice of me, I was sure. The more I thought about it, the better the idea seemed to me. I began to wonder how I could manage it. It didn't occur to me at the time that I was conforming to the things that would make me popular, instead of doing what my father wanted. The temptation to be noticed by the boys was irresistible.

I had often ridden Nellie around the farm, so that was no problem. But what could I do with the buggy?

By the time we came to Carter's Grove, I had forgotten about Pa's warning against fancy tricks. I decided that here would be a good place to leave the buggy for the day. I would put it off the road among the trees and get it on the way home.

It didn't take long to unhitch Nellie, but it was a little harder to push the buggy off the road. It was only a small one, but I wasn't very big. Nevertheless, I managed to push it to a spot where I thought it would be safe for the day, then I climbed on Nellie's back and continued on to school.

I was right about causing a stir at school. The girls all gathered around, and even some of the boys looked pretty envious. When we went in to school, the teacher mentioned it.

"Your father must trust you, Mabel, to let you come alone with the horse. You must be very careful and go straight home after school."

"Yes, Ma'am," I replied, "I will."

But I was beginning to feel ashamed of myself. Pa had trusted me, and he certainly hadn't expected that I would leave the buggy along the side of the road. However, the pleasure of having Nellie at school kept me from worrying about it for long. I would hitch up the buggy on the way home, and no one would

need to know about it.

Sarah Jane and I rode Nellie around the school ground at noon and had a wonderful time. I even hoped that Reuben and Roy would have to stay home another day so that we could do it tomorrow.

As soon as school was out, I started straight for home. I didn't know how long it would take me to get Nellie hitched to the buggy again, because I had never done it by myself before. Pa had expected that one of the boys at school would help me.

I hurried as fast as I could get Nellie to move, and soon we were back in Carter's Grove. When we reached the spot where I had left the buggy, we stopped, but I didn't get down from Nellie's back. I just sat there and looked at the trees.

The buggy was gone!

I glanced around to see if someone was playing a joke on me, but no one was in sight.

Nellie stood patiently waiting until I was ready to go on. There was no use standing in Carter's Grove any longer. Someone had obviously come along during the day and taken the buggy. Maybe they had even taken it home— and I was sure to have something waiting for me when I got there.

I was a pretty unhappy little girl. Besides

having to face Pa, the boys would hear about it and never let me forget it.

Fortunately, Pa was out in the field when I got home, and he didn't see me come in on Nellie. I put her in the barn, and quickly ran to the house. Ma was relieved to see me.

"Did you get along all right, Mabel?" she asked. "I worried about you all alone with the buggy."

I nodded and went into my room to change my clothes. Ma would really have worried if she had known that I didn't even have the buggy! I knew she would find out eventually, but it seemed better to wait as long as possible to break the news.

I was so worried about what I would tell Pa that I must have looked sick, for after awhile Ma felt my forehead.

"Dear me," she said. "I hope you aren't coming down with what the boys have. Do you feel bad?"

"No, Ma," I replied, "I feel fine. I'm a little tired, I guess."

I got busy setting the table for supper and helping Ma around the kitchen. Long before I was ready for it, Pa came in to wash.

"I see you got back safely, Mabel," he said with his face in the washdish. "You should have called me to unhitch for you. Where did you put the buggy anyway?"

"I guess I lost it, Pa," I said in a small voice.

Pa stopped splashing water and there was silence in the kitchen.

"You guess what?" he said in a puzzled voice.

"I guess I lost it," I repeated in a smaller voice.

Pa lifted his head slowly and turned to look at me in disbelief. The water ran off his beard, but he didn't seem to notice.

"Will you kindly tell me how you can lose a BUGGY?" he roared. "Nellie hasn't run fast enough to part with a buggy since she was a colt. How could you lose a buggy?"

By this time I was sobbing, and Ma was taking me on her lap.

Pa began to mop his face with the towel and stomp toward the door.

"I declare," he said, "if I had thought you could lose a buggy right out from under you, I never would have let you go this morning."

"Maryanne," he said to Ma, "how could that child possibly lose the buggy between here and the schoolhouse? I just can't believe it. Maybe you know something about girls that I don't know," he ended in disgust.

"Let's just calm down and find out what happened." Ma said. "Now, tell us, Mabel, where did you put the buggy when you got to school?"

Bit by bit I managed to sob out the story of what I had done. Pa ate his supper in silence, every so often stopping to look at me as though he couldn't believe that any daughter of his could be so foolish.

As soon as prayers were over, Pa clamped his hat on his head, and started out to find the buggy. I waited fearfully for the sound of Nellie's hoofs on the road. So far, Pa had not mentioned what my punishment was to be, but I was sure that it would not be a light one.

Finally, after what seemed hours to me, Pa returned with the buggy. He had found it, he said, in Carter's Grove. Some of the older boys had seen it there, and thinking I needed taking down a peg, pushed it into the woods a little farther. They were sure that I could find it, but since I hadn't gotten off Nellie, or looked beyond the spot where I had left it, I had not seen it.

Pa sat down and looked at me soberly.

"Mabel," he said, "since you can't seem to get over the habit of being so thoughtless, we can't let you go to school alone again. If the boys have to stay home, you'll have to stay too. Maybe when you've grown up a little more, we can trust you. But for now, you'll have to be watched like a little girl."

Then he kissed me and sent me to bed. I felt much worse than if he had paddled me good, but it certainly made me think about my foolish tricks.

Grandma looked at me with a smile.

"Now see if you can't find those mittens at school tomorrow," she said. "And try to be more careful from now on."

chapter twenty

The Spelling Bee

Sometimes when I was visiting Grandma, my things seemed to disappear. My sweater. My coloring box and crayons. Nothing seemed to be where I could find it.

"Grandma," I called as I was getting dressed one Saturday morning, "did you see my blue sweater anywhere?"

Grandma came to my bedroom door. "Did you put it away? It should be there in the drawer."

I showed her that it was not where it belonged. In fact, it was nowhere in the house.

Later, Uncle Roy came in from the barn, carrying the sweater. "I wonder if this belongs to anyone in here? It doesn't fit me."

"It's mine, Uncle Roy," I said. "I must have left it out there yesterday."

"You must have left your coloring book and crayons on the porch, too," Grandma informed me. "Last night's rain didn't do much to improve them. The sooner you

162

learn the habit of 'A place for everything and everything in its place,' the happier you'll be."

"I just forget, Grandma. Especially when I'm in a hurry to do something else."

"Maybe I should help you remember the way Pa helped us," Grandma suggested. "It didn't start out as the most pleasant lesson I ever had, but it certainly was effective."

"What was it, Grandma? Tell me, and see if I'd like it."

"I'm sure you wouldn't like it anymore than I did—to begin with," she replied. "But I'll tell you about it. . . ."

MA WAS GETTING BREAKFAST one morning as I came into the kitchen.

"Are you all ready for school, Mabel?" she asked. "If you are, you can pack the dinner pails for me. Everything is ready there on the cupboard."

I went to do as Ma instructed, and she bent over the woodbox to get more fuel for the fire.

"For goodness' sake, Mabel," she sputtered. "I almost put your speller in the stove! What in the world is it doing in the woodbox?"

"I must have left it there last night," I confessed. "I was studying by the stove."

"What if everyone in the house dropped things right where they were using them?" Ma scolded.

"We'd soon have nothing but chaos around here. Not that it doesn't come close to that anyway," she added. "Seems to me I spend half my time picking up after you children."

"I'm sorry, Ma. I'll try to do better."

Pa and the boys came in for breakfast. Pa pulled out his chair and sat down. Then just as quickly he jumped up again.

"Who spilled something on my chair?" he howled, clutching the seat of his overalls.

The boys looked at each other.

"I think you sat on my science project, Pa," Roy said. He looked at the overturned jar and wet moss on the chair. "Ruined it, too," he added. "I'll have to go back to the creek for more tadpoles."

"Tadpoles!" Ma shrieked. "Where are the ones you had in the jar?"

"Pa squashed them, I expect," Roy answered.

Ma looked grim. "You just clean that mess up before you eat breakfast. Why would you leave something like that on the chair?"

"I guess I just forgot it," Roy answered. "I'm sure I would have remembered it when I got ready to go to school."

"I'm not," Pa said. "If I hadn't sat on it, it could have stayed here until frogs were leaping around the kitchen. Don't you have anywhere in your room to keep your school doings?"

"Yes, sir," Roy replied. "But I just don't seem to get them there."

"Try," Pa said, "before I have to confiscate everything I see lying around."

"What does confiscate mean, Pa?" I asked.

"It means that when I find something out of place, I'll take it."

I thought about this as I ate breakfast. That could amount to quite a loss if it happened to be my property he found. After prayer, we gathered our books to leave for school, and Pa started out to the field. I thought I had better get something straight before he left.

"Pa, would you give it back?"

"Give what back?"

"Whatever you confiscated."

"I'll have to think about that," he said. "If you don't leave your belongings around, you won't have to know, will you?"

On the way to school, I talked it over with Sarah Jane.

"Do you think your pa would really do that?" she asked.

"I'm sure of it," I replied. "He doesn't say stuff unless he intends to do it. Once he told me that if I slammed the door one more time, he'd teach me how to close it."

"Did you slam it again?"

I nodded. "And he taught me how to close it. I opened and shut the back door for half an hour. I don't think I've slammed it since."

"Half an hour!" Sarah Jane exclaimed. "I would have cried until he let me stop."

"Then you'd still be doing it if you had my pa," I told her. "He thinks you should cry because you're sorry you did it, not because you're being punished. He can tell the difference, too!"

"I guess you'd better be careful where you put your things," Sarah Jane advised me. "You might lose something you can't live without."

I agreed, and for some time I took particular care to pick up my books and toys and clothing, and keep them out of Pa's sight. The boys were careful, too, and Ma was delighted.

"My it's nice to open a drawer and not find someone's slate pencil in among my tableware," she said. "If the suggestion works that well, we may never have to try it."

Ma was too optimistic. Unfortunately, I was the first offender.

One of the big evenings of the school year came at the end of the spring term. Parents and school board members gathered to hear reports of what had been learned during the year.

Those who excelled in mathematics worked

different problems for the visitors. The best science students prepared exhibits. There was a spelldown to choose the best speller for the year, and there were readings and recitations.

Excitement ran high the last month of school as we prepared our part of the program. This year I was to be in the spelling competition as well as give a recitation. As usual, I was concerned about what I would wear.

"Ma, do you think I could have a new dress for the program?" I asked. "I'll do extra dishes and help you if you could make me one."

"I think I saved some dimity that would make a nice dress," she said. "We'll look after supper."

The cloth was white with a small blue flower. When the dress was finished—with a ruffle on the neck and yoke—I thought it was the prettiest thing I had.

"We'll try to find a blue to match the flowers for a sash," Ma said. "I think you have the right color hair ribbons."

"Oh, Ma, it's beautiful," I sighed. "No one is going to look as pretty as I do."

"I hope you sound as good as you look. Remember, beauty is as beauty does. You can ruin the most gorgeous dress in the world by being haughty about it."

On Saturday we found the sash, and my dress

was complete for the following Friday night.

As Ma brushed my hair that evening, we talked about the program. "Do you know your piece?" she asked.

"Oh, sure, Ma. I've known it for weeks. Do you want me to say it for you?"

She nodded, and I recited the poem I had learned for the occasion.

"That's fine," she said when I had finished. "If you do your best in the spelling bee, Miss Gibson will be pleased with your work. And so will we. . . . How do your good shoes look? And did the sash match your ribbons?"

I ran to my room to get the sash and ribbons. When I picked up my shoes, I noticed a loose button on one of them.

"That sash is a good match," Ma said when I returned to the kitchen. "If you'll put those back and bring me a needle and thread, I'll fix this button. I'm glad you noticed it."

I dashed out to get what she needed. While Ma worked on my shoe, I sat down at the table to read.

"It's all finished," Ma announced. "Don't forget to take these thing back to your room."

"I won't, Ma," I assured her. "I'm almost through with this story."

I was still reading when the boys came out to the kitchen.

"We would like to get our baths if you don't mind, your highness," Reuben said. "How about going to your own room now?"

"I don't have a lamp in my room," I protested. "I only have two more pages. Can't I finish while you get your bath ready?"

"Go ahead," Reuben answered. "But be quick about it. And don't forget to take your stuff with you when you go."

"Thanks, Reuben," I said, and went back to my book. I was through in a few moments. Tucking my book under my arm, I hurried off to bed. I didn't remember my clothes until I was snuggled down under the covers.

I can't get them now, I thought. *I'll do it the first thing in the morning.* And I promptly fell asleep.

The next day was sunny and beautiful. I sang to myself as I dressed for church. After I had fastened my one shoe, I felt around under the bed with my foot for the other shoe. Suddenly I recalled where I had left it. Quickly I hopped to the kitchen door.

"Ma, would you please hand me my shoe?"

Ma looked up from the stove. "Where did you leave it?" she asked quietly.

I looked at the chair I had been sitting on the night before. The shoe was not under it. My heart sank.

"Did Pa confiscate my things?" I asked timidly.

"Yes, he did," said a voice behind me. It was Pa.

"But Pa, this is Sunday!" I pleaded.

"I'm aware of that"

"I can't go to church with one shoe on!"

"Why, no," Pa said. 1 wouldn't make you do that. You'll have to wear your school shoes to church."

My mouth dropped open in disbelief. "Ma!" I wailed. "I can't wear my everyday shoes to church!"

"You haven't much choice," Ma replied. "You only have one good shoe."

I turned and raced back to my room, sobbing loudly. I wouldn't even go to church. In fact, I wouldn't eat breakfast with the family. The boys would laugh, and everyone at church would see my old shoes.

By the time Ma called me for breakfast, I had decided not to add disobedience to my other errors. I came quitely to the table—with my school shoes on.

I ate silently, an occasional tear dripping into my bowl. Surprisingly, the boys were sympathetic.

"Pa, did you think about whether you'd give back our things if you found them?" Roy asked.

"Yes," Pa nodded. "I thought about it. I

decided I'd return them to you on your birthday."

My spoon dropped with a clatter. "But, Pa! My birthday isn't until June! What about the program?"

"I'm sorry, Mabel," Pa said gently. "But you were reminded, weren't you?"

I nodded. I had been reminded at least three times.

"Do you think I should go back on my word?"

I shook my head miserably. I was upset, but I knew Pa was being fair. I cried a lot that week, especially when I remembered that I wouldn't be able to wear my new dress, either, because Pa had my sash and ribbon.

On Friday evening, we dressed for the program before supper. Ma put a big towel around my neck while I ate.

"Just a precaution," she explained. "You are getting better about spilling."

I was nervous about the evening, and chattered more than I ate. When prayers were over, I began to help Ma clear the table.

"Mabel," Pa said, "come over here, please."

Surprised, I went over to stand in front of him.

"I'm going to give you your shoe and sash so you may wear your new dress tonight."

I couldn't have been more astounded. I had never known Pa to go back on his word.

"But why, Pa?"

"Because I love you," he said simply. "I want you to know that there is a time for justice and a time for mercy. God doesn't give us the blessings of life because we deserve them, but because he loves us. Could I do less for my little daughter?"

"Oh, Pa!" I cried, and threw my arms around his neck.

He hugged me tightly for a moment. "Here, here," he said, "we haven't much time. Roy, let me work on your hair, and, Reuben, you hitch up Nellie, please."

We all hurried to finish getting ready. That evening was as nice as any I can remember.

chapter twenty-one

Really Responsible

"Ma, why didn't you have two more daughters instead of sons?"

We were canning vegetables, and I was in charge of boiling the jars. Ma stirred the tomatoes before she answered.

"I didn't have much choice about that," she told me. "I'm thankful to have one daughter. Sons are pretty nice to have, too."

"I can't think what for," I retorted. "Why don't they have to stand over a hot stove once in a while?"

"For the same reason you don't spend the days in the field with Pa, or milk the cows night and morning. It's called a division of labor."

"Not a very fair division, if you ask me," I grumbled. "I'd rather be outdoors in the fresh air and sunshine."

"All right. I'll watch those jars and you go get

173

some peas and lettuce from the garden," Ma offered. "It's time to start dinner."

"That's not what I had in mind."

"I know!" Ma replied dryly. "What you had in mind was sitting on the fence, gazing out across the field. But that doesn't run a farm."

While I washed the lettuce at the pump and shelled the peas, I dreamed about what I might be doing in five years. My dreams definitely didn't include a farm.

"I think I'd like to go far, far away," I announced to Ma as I carried the pans into the kitchen.

"You've already been far, far away," she said. "You should be able to separate the pods from the peas better than this."

"I was thinking of my future," I told her.

"If your future is anything like your present, you're going to need a caretaker," Ma retorted. "I wish you'd learn to keep your mind on your work. Can't you see that it takes twice as long to do a job over again?"

Later Sarah Jane dropped in, and we sat on the porch to talk.

"I've been making plans for my future," I said. "There aren't a whole lot of things a girl can do, but I'd like to do all of them."

"How many lives are you planning on living?"

Sarah Jane answered. "I'd be glad to think of one thing I'd like to do."

I looked at her thoughtfully. "Your biggest talent is telling me when I'm wrong," I said. "There must be some way you could build that into a career." I ducked as she swatted at me.

"What are all these things you want to do?" she asked.

"I could teach school, or maybe be a nurse, or—"

"Or you could get married," Sarah Jane finished for me. "I think your best choice is right there. You could be a farmer's wife or minister's wife or storekeeper's wife or—"

"No, no," I interrupted her. "I've been somebody's daughter this far in my life, and I don't want to be somebody's wife the rest of it. I want to be successful on my own. I'd like to have a really responsible place in life."

Sarah Jane shook her head. "You're dreaming, Mabel. That would mean you'd be in charge of something. Can't you imagine what a disaster that would be?"

"Sarah Jane! I don't discourage you when you tell me about your dreams!"

"Of course not," she replied. "I don't want to try anything I'm not able to accomplish. What you have to do is suit your ambitions to your

175

capabilities. When you get older, you'll thank me for my advice."

"Just don't stand on one foot until I do." I retorted.

But when I reported the conversation to Ma that evening, I admitted the truth of Sarah Jane's remarks. "That's the maddening thing about Sarah Jane—she's usually right."

"You've improved somewhat over the years," Ma told me. "But you have a ways to go. I appreciate every little bit of progress."

"I've never had any big responsibility to see if I could handle it, Ma. How does anyone know what I'd do?"

"Do you remember the parable of the talents that Jesus told? The master said that when the servant was faithful over a little, he would receive much. You have to prove yourself in small things, and then you'll be trusted with large ones."

"From now on, I'm going to be a responsible person," I declared. "I'll show everyone!"

"Responsible for what?" Roy asked as he came into the kitchen. "Seems to me you're already responsible for everything that goes wrong around here. What more do you want?"

"Now, Roy," Ma warned.

"I'll ignore that," I said.

A few days later, Ma asked me to sew some buttons on Pa's shirt.

"Sure," I replied. "Just as soon as I finish this chapter." I took the buttons and slipped them into my apron pocket. Before I had reached the end of the page, Sarah Jane arrived with some exciting news.

"How would you like to take a trip to Eastman with me?" she asked. "We're going to leave on the early morning train and come back on the evening one. We'll have all day to look around town and have a picnic in the park. Won't that be fun?"

"I'd love to," I exclaimed. "I think Ma would let me go. What day will it be?"

"Friday," Sarah Jane replied. "The day after tomorrow."

"That would be a nice trip," Ma said when we asked her. "It was kind of your folks to invite Mabel to share the day with you. Will you be taking the seven-thirty train?"

"Yes, ma'am," Sarah Jane replied. "And Mabel won't need to bring anything. Ma will have enough lunch for all of us."

"Perhaps you could pick up some yard goods and thread for me, Mabel," Ma said. "That is, if you aren't having such a good time you forget it."

"I told you I was going to be more reliable," I replied. "Of course I won't forget it."

Sarah Jane and I went outside to talk about the trip.

"You shouldn't be promising things like being more reliable," she said. "You know how easy it is for you to have something on your mind and not remember stuff."

"If you weren't my best friend, I wouldn't have anything to do with you," I said. "Don't you think people can change for the better?"

"Certainly 'people' can," Sarah Jane replied. "It's just you that I don't have much hope for. But never mind, I'll help you remember what your ma wants."

I didn't have to be called on Friday morning; I was up as soon as I heard Ma in the kitchen. My good dress and shoes were ready to put on, but I would wait until after breakfast to get dressed. As I set the table, I went over what Ma had asked for.

"You want six yards of a pretty blue print, eight yards of white shirting, and three spools of white thread. Is that right?"

"Yes," Ma said, "that's it. I'll surely be glad to have it. Pa and the boys need shirts in the worst way. Which reminds me—Pa is going to town this morning, and the only shirt he has to wear is the one you sewed buttons on the other day. Where did you put it?"

"I'll go see," I said hurriedly. "I think it's in my room."

I knew it was in my room, hanging over my chair. But where were the buttons? I didn't have much time to find them and get them sewed on. I couldn't tell Ma that I'd forgotten about it. Frantically I tried to remember what I had been doing when she gave them to me.

"Mabel," Ma called. "You'd better hurry if you're going to eat. Here's Sarah Jane coming up the steps now." But I couldn't find them anyplace.

I looked everywhere I thought the buttons could be, and then went back and looked again. I could hear Ma and Sarah Jane talking in the kitchen, and I knew I couldn't stay in my room forever. Reluctantly I took the shirt and went out to face Ma.

"You've either done something you shouldn't or you haven't done something you should," Sarah Jane said with a sigh. "I can tell by the look on your face."

"I didn't sew the buttons on Pa's shirt and now I don't know where they are," I blurted.

"I'm not surprised," Ma replied. "I thought when I saw you put those buttons in your pocket that they'd be out of sight, out of mind."

179

"Oh! That's right! They're in my apron. But I won't have time to do what I was supposed to and still go. It's my fault, I can't blame anyone else." I looked imploringly at Ma. "Would you do it for me, just this once if I promise not to forget again?"

Ma looked sorry, but she shook her head. "I don't think I will, Mabel. I'm afraid there's no other way for you to learn than to repair your own mistakes."

I nodded and went back to my room to get the buttons. I couldn't help crying as I thought of the beautiful day we had planned. It was all spoiled, and it was my own fault.

When I returned to the kitchen, Sarah Jane was still sitting at the table. I wiped my eyes, sat down, and jabbed at a button.

"You'd better hurry up," I said to her. "There's no sense in both of us missing the trip."

"Shall I tell her before she finishes that job?" Sarah Jane asked Ma.

"Tell me what?"

"I just came by to let you know that we can't go this morning because Pa hurt his foot. We're going tomorrow instead. Now aren't you glad you have another opportunity to prove how reliable you can be? You won't get a second chance every time, you know."

"I'm sorry your pa hurt his foot, but I'm glad I can go. And who knows, Sarah Jane? I might live long enough to become as upright and virtuous as you are."

"Never mind," she said with a grin. "I'm willing to do anything I can to help you improve. After all, you are my best friend!"

chapter twenty-two

Grandpa's Apron

"Look here, Grandma," I said. "This square is awfully heavy. What was it from?"

Grandma and I were tying her big quilt, and many of the big squares had yielded a good story. Grandma looked, and then a twinkle came to her eye.

"Well, now," she said. "That was a pocket from your Grandpa's apron."

"Grandpa's apron! Did Grandpa really have his own apron?" I giggled.

"He certainly did," Grandma laughed. "And you aren't the first one who thought that was funny!"

"Tell me about it, Grandma," I said.

So Grandma began. . . .

GRANDPA CAME HOME FROM TOWN ONE DAY with this big heavy piece of goods. He said he wanted an apron made for himself—a very special apron. That evening he drew a picture of it for me, and together we cut a pattern out of paper. It was a special apron, too. It had a pocket for everything Grandpa wanted with him.

There was a pocket to hold Scripture verses, written on cards. These verses were pulled out and recited to Nellie and Bess while Grandpa milked in the morning and at night.

There was a deeper pocket that held a small song book. It was propped on the stall and Grandpa sang all the verses of "How Firm A Foundation" or "O This Uttermost Salvation" to the stock as he fed and watered them.

Sermon notes were in another pocket. They came out as Grandpa followed behind the plow, and the horses were treated to next Sunday's sermon while they walked up and down the rows.

One little pocket in a handy place held round, pink wintergreen drops with small x's on them. Another had a selection of nails that often came in handy. There was room for a fresh cookie or a piece of homemade bread and butter. I'm not sure I ever knew what was in all those pockets, but Grandpa did.

It was a funny-looking apron, to be sure, and Grandpa took a lot of good-natured teasing about it. My brother Reuben would say, "Here comes Len in his milk-maid's apron. Do you suppose the cows would give any milk if he forgot to wear it?"

Or Roy would say, "Oh, Len, do you have an empty pocket in your apron to carry my tools to the back field?"

Grandpa would laugh along with them, but he would say, "I hope you boys notice that I don't make a dozen trips to the house or barn while I'm working. I have everything right where I need it."

And so Grandpa continued to replenish his pockets and wear this apron as he went about his chores. But a day was to come when no one laughed at Grandpa's apron.

One afternoon in the fall, Grandpa was working in the hayloft, repairing the floor before the new hay came in. Somehow his foot slipped on a crossbeam, and he started to fall. His apron flew out and caught on the hook that was used to lift the bales to the loft, and Grandpa hung suspended many feet over the concrete barn floor.

He began to pray loudly for the Lord to send someone to the barn. The Lord heard him. So did Reuben and Roy, who ran to the barn door to find the reason for such loud prayers.

Quickly they pushed the hay-wagon under Grandpa and began to lower the haylift, with Grandpa still attached to it, onto the wagon bed.

"You boys get me down from here," Grandpa shouted, "and maybe I can talk Mabel into making

you an apron like this!"

As they loosened the hook from Grandpa's apron, Reuben exclaimed, "What in the world kept that hook from going clean to the bottom of this silly apron?"

"Why, the Lord did, of course," Grandpa responded. "And now maybe you clowns will have a little more respect for this valuable piece of goods."

He stalked to the house, leaving Reuben and Roy to contemplate the distance that he would have fallen to the barn floor, had not the Lord—and his apron—held him securely.

I mended the apron, and Grandpa continued to keep it stocked and in use. The boys didn't laugh again. They knew they had seen a miracle that day.

Grandma laughed and patted the square on the quilt.

"That sure was a strong piece of goods," she said. "And you wouldn't be here to listen to the story if your Grandpa hadn't been wearing it that afternoon!"

chapter twenty-three

The Prettiest House in the County

Grandma, Uncle Roy, and I were sitting around the kitchen table in the old farmhouse.

We had just sampled some gingerbread,hot from the oven, and I was listening to Grandma and her brother as they talked about the farm.

"The house really could stand some paint,Roy," Grandma said. "How long since it's been done?"

Uncle Roy's eyes twinkled as he replied. "It's been painted since the barn has."

Grandma began to laugh, and I knew that they both had remembered something from their childhood.

"Tell me!" I begged. "What happened that was funny?"

"I have to get back out to work, so you'll have to tell her, Mabel!" Uncle Roy insisted.

Grandma got up to clear the table and began the story. . . .

I WAS ABOUT NINE YEARS OLD when Ma began to campaign for the house to be painted. We had lived in this house since Pa moved us from the log cabin when I was only four years old. It had not been repainted since then.

"Aren't you just a little bit ashamed of the way this house looks?" she asked Pa. "The paint is peeling dreadfully."

"Why, no," Pa replied innocently. "I hadn't noticed that it looked too bad. In fact, it looks pretty good to me."

Ma sniffed. "It would look good to you if it were falling down around your ears."

"Well, I wouldn't go so far as to say that," Pa replied. "I think I'd notice if it fell in on me."

From time to time, Ma continued to hint that new paint would be acceptable to her. Pa either didn't hear, or chose to ignore her. Finally, as spring gave way to summer, Ma seemed to be getting someplace.

"The garden is in and the spring rains have about ended," she announced one morning. "Do you think the weather will hold for a couple of weeks?"

"I wouldn't be surprised," Pa replied. "The almanac doesn't predict any rain for the rest of this month. Things are growing well, though. We need the sunny days for the wheat."

"Then this would be an excellent time to paint!" Ma declared triumphantly.

Pa looked out the window. "You know, I think you're right. Maybe I could get a couple of the Carter boys to help me. I think I can pick up the paint while I'm in town Saturday. I wonder how much it will take?"

Ma's mouth dropped open in surprise. She had obviously expected some excuse.

"I'm sure Mr. Clapp could tell you how much you'll need," she said happily. "You can start right away on Monday. What color will you get? . . . I think white or pale yellow would look pretty."

"Um, yes," Pa murmured. "We'll see. I'll take care of it."

As Ma and I cleared the breakfast dishes off the table we discussed the painting.

"I think yellow with white trim would look good," I suggested.

"I'll settle for anything Pa brings," Ma replied. "I'm so tired of seeing the place look like no one cared about it."

"I can help Pa," I offered. "It's a good thing school is out so I'll be right here."

"I'm sure the men won't want you hanging around," Ma replied.

"Oh, Ma! I'd be careful. I could paint the back where it won't be seen from the road."

"I'd just as soon my house looked as nice from the back as it does from the front, thank you. It won't be any job for a little girl."

I was disappointed, but I knew that Ma's word was law. However, I determined to stay close and watch. It wasn't every day that something exciting happened on our farm.

"We get to help paint," Roy announced at suppertime. "Pa says we're big enough to be of some use around here."

"I'm glad to hear it," Ma said. "You can fill up the reservoir with water after supper. Reuben, you can bring in more wood. That will be very useful."

The boys groaned and Pa chuckled. "Guess you'll be careful what you say from now on. Ma can keep you busy anytime you're available."

On Saturday, Pa loaded the wagon with a plow to be sharpened and a harness that needed a new buckle, and left for town. I couldn't keep my mind on my chores for watching the road.

"He hasn't had time to get there yet, let alone buy paint and get back. Patience certainly isn't one of your virtues, is it?" Ma remarked.

"I'm just excited about it, that's all. I can see how nice it's going to look."

"I can, too," Ma said. "I guess all my prodding

did some good. Although I must admit, I'm surprised he gave in without more of a struggle."

Ma and I ate dinner alone. Then she suggested that I run over to see Sarah Jane for the afternoon.

"I guess I'd better not. I might not get back before Pa does. I want to be here when he brings the paint."

However, I was helping Ma put supper on the table when Pa and the boys drove in. They went directly to the barn and unloaded the wagon; then they came to the house to wash.

"Did you get it, Pa?" I clamored. "Did you get all the paint? Will you be ready to start on Monday?"

Pa nodded. "Yes, we got it all. But I won't be able to start Monday after all. Jed Carter wants me to go with him to buy some cattle. I think I may get us another heifer."

"That's good," Ma said. "One more day won't make that much difference. What color did you get—white or yellow?"

There was no answer. Ma looked around at Pa, who had his face buried in a towel.

"James?"

Pa cleared his throat. "Well, actually, neither one."

"Neither one? I thought we had decided on those colors. What did you get, then?'

191

Pa looked uncomfortable. "Red."

"Red!" Ma cried. "Why on earth would you buy red? That's not a color for a house! The only thing that's good for is the . . ."

Ma stopped suddenly and sat down at the table. "James," she said quietly, "are you planning to paint the barn?"

Pa avoided looking directly at her. "Well, yes," he mumbled. "I thought I would."

"You said you would paint the house."

"Oh, I will. Just as soon as the barn is done. You can see how badly it needs it, can't you?" He looked appealingly at Ma.

Ma got up and went back to the stove. Something in her eye said that Pa would hear more about the matter when we children were out of earshot.

The next morning, Ma was her usual cheerful self as she bustled around the kitchen preparing breakfast and getting us ready for church. If she looked a little more determined than usual, no one seemed to notice. We climbed into the buggy and left for church.

"What time do you plan to leave tomorrow morning?" Ma asked pleasantly.

"I think as soon as it's daylight," Pa answered. "It'll take longer getting home since we have to walk the cattle."

"I'll help the boys milk in the morning so you can get ready to leave," Ma said.

When I arrived in the kitchen the following morning, the milking had been done. The breakfast was ready to go on the table, even though the sun had not yet peeped over the horizon.

"Looks like a beautiful day," Pa boomed as he sat down. "The Lord is good to us to give us such perfect growing weather."

"Yes, He is," Ma agreed. "We have a lot to be thankful for."

"You know what there is to do around here," Pa reminded the boys. "And if your Ma has any chores she wants done, you be available to do them."

"Yes, Pa," Reuben replied. "We'll take care of things."

Roy hitched Nellie to the wagon, and Pa climbed in. Ma stood at the kitchen door watching as they disappeared down the lane. Then she turned to Reuben and Roy.

"Boys, I want you to go out to the barn and fetch that paint to the house. And don't forget the brushes and the ladder."

They stared at her, dumbfounded. "What are you going to do with it, Ma?"

"I'm going to paint the house, of course."

"But, Ma," Roy protested, "that paint is for the barn!"

"It was for the barn," Ma corrected him. "It is now for the house. I'm tired of waiting for my house to be painted, and I don't intend to take second place to a barn. Now, move. And Mabel," she turned to me, "come along and put on an older dress. I don't want paint on that one."

"But Ma," I wailed as I trotted after her, "we wanted a white house! It will look just like we lived in a barn!"

"That can't be helped. I would prefer white, myself. But at least it will look clean. We can get some white to trim the windows and doors."

The boys returned with the paint and ladders, and Ma met them at the steps.

"Are we starting back here, Ma?' Reuben asked.

"Indeed not," Ma declared. "We'll begin on the front. Your father might not finish it right away if it couldn't be noticed from the road. But he won't leave the job undone when the neighbors can see it."

The boys looked at each other and shrugged. When they had carried everything around to the front, Ma directed the job.

"Now, Reuben, you set up the ladder and start at the top. Roy, you start as high as you can reach and work down. Mabel, you begin at the bottom and

194

work up. I'll paint around the windows and doors."

We went to work at once, and stopped only for a cold lunch at dinner time.

"You're doing a good job, children. If we keep it up until sundown, we should have most of the front done."

"What's Pa going to say when he gets home?" Reuben ventured to ask.

"Why, I'm sure he'll think we've done a good job," Ma replied. "It looks very nice so far, and we haven't wasted any paint."

"But he intended to do the barn with this paint," Roy put in. "Aren't you afraid he'll be mad?"

"Your father doesn't get mad," Ma declared. "Annoyed, maybe, or even put out a little, but not mad."

We went back to work after dinner, and by the time the sun set, we had made a noticeable difference in the front of the house. Ma stood back and admired it.

"Now I call that a good day's work," she said proudly. "You see how much better the house looks with a little paint?"

"It certainly looks . . . red," Reuben agreed. "We'll be able to see it from a long way off."

"I like it, Ma," I said loyally. "It looks a lot better."

"All right, boys. We'll stop for now. Put the

things away and start your chores. I'll help you milk again this evening. You've been good assistants."

The boys left to get the cows, and Ma and I went inside to begin supper.

"Do you suppose Pa will be home before dark?" I asked. "If he isn't, he won't see it until tomorrow."

"I don't know," Ma said. "But I think we can start looking for him anytime now."

Supper was all ready, and it was dark before we heard the sound of the wagon on the lane. I could imagine Pa brushing and feeding Nellie, putting the new cow in her stall, and then heading for the house.

Soon the back door opened, and Pa came in.

Ma greeted him with a smile. "Did you have a successful day?"

"Yes, we did. Brought home a fine heifer."

He sat down and looked at Ma. The corners of his mouth twitched as he tried to keep from laughing. "I guess you've had a pretty busy day, too. Haven't you?"

"Yes. We've been working around the house ever since you left."

Pa burst out laughing. "I can't see it, but I can smell it. I had it coming to me. How does it look?"

"Very fine, indeed," Ma replied. "As soon as

you bring enough white for the trim, it will be the prettiest house in the county."

"It will be the brightest, anyway," Pa chuckled. "The Carters will be here tomorrow to help finish it. . . ."

"We got used to our bright red house," Grandma concluded. "In fact, we all rather liked that color. And Pa learned that when Ma had her heart set on something, she would probably get it!"

chapter twenty-four

Gypsies!

"WHEW! I DON'T THINK IT'S EVER BEEN this hot before!" Sarah Jane exclaimed.

"You say that every summer," I replied. "I try to think about something cool and not pay attention to the heat."

"It doesn't do you much good," Sarah Jane retorted. "Your face looks like a pickled beet."

We sat under the big tree at the end of our lane, facing the dry and dusty road. The heat seemed to rise from it in waves.

Suddenly an unusual contraption appeared around the curve. It looked like a house on wheels. The sides of the wagon bed were built up, and a canvas was stretched over the top for a roof. A dark-haired man walked beside the horse, and a woman with a shawl over her head sat in the doorway at the back of the wagon. Two little boys ran along behind.

We watched silently until the strange apparition disappeared from sight.

"Did you see that, Mabel?" Sarah Jane asked. I nodded.

"Good," she said. "I thought maybe the heat was getting to me the way they say it does on the desert, when you start seeing things."

"A mirage," I said.

"A what?"

"A mirage. That's what you see on a desert. Only I don't think it looks like a wagon. Who do you suppose they are?"

"I don't know," Sarah Jane answered. "I've never seen them before. Do you imagine they live in that wagon?"

"There's not room enough in there to live," I replied. "Where would they cook and eat and do the washing?"

"It looked to me like they had all they owned on there. I saw cooking pots and clothes and everything."

"Maybe they're moving from one farm to another," I suggested.

"I don't think so," she disagreed. "There wasn't room for furniture in there. I think they live in it."

"Gypsies," Pa said when we told him what we had seen. "They're a group of wandering people.

199

They stay awhile in one place, and then they move on."

"They'll steal you blind, too," Roy chimed in.

Pa looked at him sternly. "That's not fair to say. Not all Gypsies are thieves, just because an occasional one takes something. There are dishonest people in every walk of life, you know."

Reuben returned from town with the announcement that the Gypsies were camped in the Gibbs's back pasture, next to the creek.

"Is it just one wagon?" Pa asked. "Usually they travel in caravans."

"Just one," Reuben replied. "It doesn't look like a very large family. I only saw two children."

"What do they do for a living?" I asked Pa. "How can they work if they don't live in one place very long?"

"Some of the men are silversmiths," Pa told me.

"And I've seen beautiful handwork the women do," Ma said. "I don't think I'd want to be on the go all the time, though. I feel more comfortable on a piece of land that belongs to me and in a house that stands still."

"I'd like it," I said. "Think of all the places you'd see."

"If you've seen one back road, you've seen them all," Roy said. "And besides, Gypsies aren't very well liked. You'd get pretty lonesome."

Sarah Jane agreed when I discussed it with her
the next morning.

"You couldn't live in a wagon, Mabel. There
wouldn't be room enough for all your stuff.
You've still got the wood chips we used for dishes
when we played house."

"They are memorabilia," I told her loftily. "I
wouldn't take everything I owned with me. Just
the necessities."

"You'd have to stop off here once a month to
leave the memorabilia you collected along the
road."

We talked about walking down to the Gibbs's
to see if the family was still there, but decided
against it.

"It's not that we're afraid of them," I said to Ma
as we did the dinner dishes. "But we didn't want
them to think we were spying on them."

"That was sensible," Ma said. "I think they like
to keep pretty much to themselves."

We were in for a surprise the next morning.
When Ma opened the back door to call Pa and the
boys to breakfast, she just missed hitting a little
gypsy boy who was standing on the porch. "Oh,
mercy!" Ma exclaimed. "You startled me! Have you
been here long?"

The boy shook his head and said, "Baby sick.
You come?"

"Of course," Ma replied promptly. Quickly she turned, and as she buttered some biscuits and put ham on them, she instructed me to go ahead with breakfast. Before Pa got to the house, she was sailing down the lane with the little boy running to keep up with her.

"Do you think Ma should have gone over there by herself?" Reuben worried.

"Ma can take care of herself," Pa replied. "When someone is sick, you know she'll go."

"But, Gypsies, Pa," Roy said. "They aren't—"

"Gypsies are people, Roy. They live differently, but they have the same needs everyone else has. God loves them as much as He does us. You know your ma doesn't ask people for their pedigree if they need help."

That closed the matter, but even Pa was surprised a little later to see the gypsy wagon turning down our lane.

I watched open-mouthed as Ma jumped down from the back of the wagon, and then reached up to take a shawl-wrapped bundle from the gypsy woman.

"Mabel, fill the small tub with water, please. Put in just enough hot to take off the chill."

I scurried to do as Ma requested, and Pa went out to the wagon.

"This is Mr. Romani," Ma told him. "They were

on the way to Canada when the baby took sick.
Come, Mrs. Romani. We'll take care of her."

Ma soon had the baby unwrapped from the
shawl and many layers of clothing. She sponged
the feverish little body with tepid water. Mrs.
Romani looked frightened, but she allowed Ma to
do whatever she wanted to with the baby.

"I'll fix some warm water with sugar and just a
drop of peppermint," Ma told her. "Then I think
you should both lie down and get some sleep."

"I'd have a fever, too, if I had all that wrapped
around me in this weather." I spoke to Ma after
the Romanis had been settled in the spare room.

Ma nodded. "I know. They think babies should
be wrapped up tight to keep the evil spirits away.
I don't think it's anything more than summer colic,
but she was so worried. It will be easier to look
after them here than to run back and forth to the
Gibbs's pasture."

The next couple of days were interesting, to
say the least. The Romanis did not want to come
into the house to eat, so we ate outside. Pa set up
one of the tables we used when threshers were
here, and Ma made it plain that our guests were to
eat with us. They listened quietly while Pa read
the Bible and we prayed. We couldn't tell whether
they understood or not, but Pa assured us that
God's Word would not return to Him without

accomplishing what it set out to do.

Mrs. Romani timidly offered to help, and Ma gave her tasks that she could do while she watched the baby. The little boys picked raspberries, and Pa reported that Mr. Romani was mending harnesses and sharpening tools in the barn.

"Are you going to ask the Romanis to go to church with us?" I asked Ma on Sunday morning.

Ma considered that for a moment. "No," she said finally. "I don't think they would be comfortable in an unfamiliar place. I don't know how they worship God, but they don't need curious people staring at them."

Pa told Mr. Romani that we would return shortly after noon, and we left for the service.

Ma had no sooner alighted from the buggy than she was surrounded by neighboring ladies.

"Maryanne, do you mean to say that you've had those Gypsies in your yard all week?"

"Weren't you afraid to go to sleep at night?"

"Could you understand what they said?"

"Did you leave them there alone while you came to church today?"

Ma answered each question pleasantly, but it was plain to see that she was not saying all she felt. I was glad when Pa returned from staking Nellie and we went into the church.

Ma's face was pretty grim as we turned toward home.

"I declare, I don't understand people," she said. "Anyone should be willing to take in a needy family if they have the means. Why would we be afraid of a nice young couple like that?"

"Gypsies have a poor reputation," Pa replied. "No one wants to trust someone who has no roots and no hometown. People feel better about a person if they know his grandfather."

"Hmph," Ma sniffed. "I've known some respectable people whose grandfathers were horse thieves."

We had only to turn into our lane to see that the Romanis' wagon was gone.

The dire predictions of our neighbors were in our thoughts as we approached the house, but no one had the bad judgment to voice them to Ma. We didn't have to.

"I know what you're thinking," she said to us, "and you're wrong. The Romanis would not take anything from us. And even if they did, it doesn't change the fact that people are more important than things. They needed help, and we gave it. We'll do it again when the opportunity arises."

The house was quiet as we entered, and everything was in its accustomed place. It was as though there had never been a gypsy family there.

Ma took the pot roast from the oven, and I went to change my dress. The door of the spare room was open and I glanced in as I walked by.

"Ma!" I called. "Come and see!"

Ma and Pa both joined me, and the boys were close behind.

"Why, did you ever!" Ma breathed.

On the bed lay three gold coins, two silver belt buckles, a bolt of cloth, and a beautiful white lace shawl.

"They needn't have done that," Ma said. "They might have used the money these things would bring."

"I think they figured they got more than money," Reuben said. "They knew you loved them, Ma. That's more important than things, too, isn't it?"

"Yes, it is," Ma said, brushing tears from her eyes. "It certainly is."

chapter twenty-five

The Dog Who Could Spell

One afternoon as Grandma and I were looking at some old pictures in her album, I noticed something strange. There were no casual photographs like the ones I was used to seeing. They all looked as though they had been taken in a studio.

"Most of our pictures were," Grandma said when I pointed this out to her. "Families didn't usually have cameras of their own. They were too expensive. Often visiting photographers came around to take our pictures."

She turned one of the photographs over. "Some of them were printed on postcards that could be sent through the mail. Like this one. But most of our pictures were on heavy cardboard for framing or mounting in an album.

"We didn't have a lot of pictures taken, but I think we have some of everyone in the family."

"I wish you had one of Pep," I said. "He really was a nice old dog, wasn't he?"

"We thought so," Grandma agreed. "All of us talked to him as though he could understand every word we said. Come to think of it," she added, "I believe he did know what we were talking about. He was just like a little child, though. If it didn't suit him to understand, he wouldn't. If it was to his advantage, he had no trouble at all.

"Ma would sometimes get awfully annoyed with him—especially when he tracked up her floor or tried to sneak into the boys' room. But I remember one time when she actually hugged him!"

"He must have done something pretty special," I said. "What was it?"

Grandma eased back in her rocking chair, and I knew she would tell me another story. . . .

WHEN IT WAS COLD, Pep was allowed to sleep on a rug beside the stove. Ma wasn't entirely in favor of that arrangement. But the boys and I pleaded his cause, and Pa was on our side.

"He doesn't take up much room," he said. "As long as he behaves himself I don't see why he shouldn't stay in at night, now that he's getting older."

So Ma consented, and we were pleased. Pep seemed to know that his good fortune depended upon his behavior. He was a model dog on cold winter nights.

One evening in late fall, we were sitting around the supper table. Pep was lying on his rug near the stove. He had his nose between his paws, and he appeared to be asleep. Reuben looked at him fondly.

"Do you remember when we brought Pep home?" he asked Ma.

"Brought him home?" I asked. "I don't remember when he wasn't already here."

Reuben looked disgusted. "Of course you don't, silly. You were only two years old. We didn't even live in this house then."

Ma laughed. "You can be sure I remember. I almost killed the poor thing before I knew what it was."

"Oh, Ma!" I gasped. "How could you?"

"It certainly wasn't on purpose. The boys had been down the road to the Gibbs's place. Reuben was only about six years old. When Mr. Gibbs offered him a puppy, he accepted happily. He never thought to ask about it."

"That's right," Reuben put in. "The puppy was so small and cute; I just knew we had to have him."

A thump on the floor told us that Pep was listening, even though he didn't open his eyes.

Reuben continued. "On the way home Roy mentioned that Ma might not let us keep him. I hadn't even thought of that. But the closer we got to home, the more likely it seemed.

"I decided to get him in the house without Ma seeing him. We could save enough from our meals to feed him, and we could keep him hidden in our room."

"The boys slept up in the loft," Ma explained, "above the kitchen. Somehow Reuben managed to sneak that puppy up the ladder and into the loft. That evening when it was time for Pa and me to go to bed, I went up the ladder with a light. I always checked to be sure the boys were covered. I set the light down by the bed, and leaned over to pull Reuben's quilts up. Suddenly, the blankets at the foot of his bed began to bob up and down.

" 'Oh, James!' I hollered. 'Come quick! There's a rat in Reuben's bed!'

"I grabbed the first thing that came to hand, and began beating on the lump in the bed. If there hadn't been so many covers over him, I would have knocked that poor dog senseless.

"Pa came running up the ladder and yanked back the quilts. There was that puppy, looking so woebegone that I almost cried. Of course Reuben was wide awake by now. He howled so loudly that Roy woke up and joined in. If we'd had any close neighbors, I'm sure they would all have been there.

"Finally," Ma said, "everyone was settled down. There was no way I could get rid of the pup after scaring the wits out of him. So we put him in a box by the stove. He's been with us ever since."

"There have been times," Pa chuckled, "when your ma thought maybe she did knock all the sense out of him. Sometimes he doesn't act too bright."

"Oh, no, Pa," I protested. "Pep is awfully smart. He even knows how to spell!"

"That's right," Reuben agreed. "He really does."

"Now that I'd like to see," Ma said skeptically. "I'll admit he's smart enough to know that it's warmer inside by the stove, but he can't spell."

"You watch," Reuben told her. "Pa, may I have that b-o-n-e for P-e-p?"

Pep's ears picked up, and his tail thumped loudly on the floor. He gave a happy woof and looked expectantly toward the table.

"Well, what do you know!" Pa exclaimed. "He acts as though he knows what you spelled."

Ma had to agree that Pep showed some intelligence, and the dog was soon gnawing contentedly on his bone.

The next morning Sarah Jane arrived with her doll, and I ran to get my doll, Emily. Ma asked us to gather a basket of nuts for her.

"This is probably the last time we can get nuts," she said as she handed a basket to us. "It's going to snow soon."

We agreed, and took the basket, swinging it happily between us. Pep tagged along, pausing now and then to sniff through a pile of leaves or run ahead as he spied a squirrel in the path.

"I sure do like Saturdays," Sarah Jane said. "Isn't it fun to just walk through the leaves and not be in a hurry to go somewhere?"

"Yes, and I'd like it even better if we had a picnic lunch and could stay all day. But it's too cold for that now. By the time we get the nuts picked up, we'll be ready to start back."

"How come Pep knows this is Saturday?" Sarah Jane wondered. "He never follows us to school, and we start out this same way. Do you think he can tell time?"

"I wouldn't be surprised," I replied. "He's a very smart dog. Do you want to see how he can spell?"

"No dog is that smart," Sarah Jane declared. "He can't even talk."

"That's not the way he does it," I explained. "Look, I'll show you." I picked up a stick from the ground and held it over my head. "Here, Pep! Go fetch the s-t-i-c-k." I threw it as far as I could, and Pep galloped after it, happy to have something to chase. He brought it back to me, and I turned triumphantly to Sarah Jane. "See?"

"Oh, Mabel! He'd have brought that back if you had said, 'go fetch the h-o-u-s-e!' That doesn't prove that he can spell. It just proves he likes to play games."

"Anyway, he's smart. Smarter than any dog I ever had."

"You never had another one," Sarah Jane pointed out.

"Are you trying to say that Pep is dumb?" I demanded. "Everything I say, you argue with me."

"I won't argue anymore," Sarah Jane promised. "Here, this tree has lots of nuts under it. Let's start here."

We set the basket down and propped the two dolls up under the tree.

"I think we can get the basket full in half an hour," I predicted. "There's a butternut tree over there, too, when we finish here."

We worked quickly, partly because we were in a hurry to get home for the cookies Ma had promised us as a reward, and partly because it was getting much colder.

"Oh, look, Sarah Jane! See what I found!" I pointed to the maple tree near us. "There's a little clump of mistletoe up there. Let's get it, shall we?"

"I'll watch you get it," she replied. "You know I

can't climb a tree if I have to take my feet off the ground."

"You can't climb anything if you don't take your feet off the ground," I said. "How come you're not afraid of falling out of bed at night?"

"That's different. The bed is wider than a tree limb. I just stay away from the edge."

"Well, that isn't very far up," I decided. "I'll go up after it. Stand right there, and I'll drop it down to you."

The mistletoe was farther out than I had thought so it took a while to work my way toward the end of the branch.

"Oh, Mabel!" Sarah Jane squeaked. "You can't pick that mistletoe and hang onto the branch at the same time! You'd better come down."

"I'll hang on with one hand," I replied. But I was not able to do that. My other hand slipped, and I plunged to the ground. I landed on my stomach, with my arm bent under me. The wind was knocked out of me, and I lay still with my eyes closed.

"I didn't mean for you to come down that way!" Sarah Jane screamed. "Mabel, are you dead?"

When I could get my breath, I assured her that I was not. But I was hurt.

"I'd better go get your Pa," Sarah Jane said anxiously. "I can't carry you home."

"No, I'd rather have you stay here with me. I'll send Pep back for help. Pep," I called to him, "go home and get Pa. Hurry!"

"Mabel! For goodness' sake! You must have fallen on your head. That dog can't tell anyone what happened. Look there. He thinks you're playing another game."

It surely did look that way. After circling around me a few times, Pep grabbed Emily in his mouth and turned to run toward home.

"I'll wait just a few minutes; then I'm going myself," Sarah Jane declared. "It's too cold for you to be lying here on the ground."

By this time I was able to pull myself up and lean against the tree. I was sure my arm was broken, and I knew my knee was too sore to walk. But I was confident that Pep would get the message home, and help would be on the way.

When Pep dashed up on our porch at home, Ma was working at the stove. He scratched on the door, but Ma didn't turn around.

"You don't come in at this time of day," she said to him. "Go on about your business."

Pep turned and ran to the barn. Reuben met him at the door.

"What are you doing with Mabel's doll? You're going to be in trouble if you lose that. Here, give it to me."

Pep refused to give up the doll. Instead he turned and ran a short way, and then stopped. When Reuben started after him, he kept just a few feet ahead, looking back to be sure he was being followed.

"Pa," Reuben called, "I think something has happened to Mabel. Pep has her doll in his mouth, and he acts like he wants us to follow him."

It wasn't long before we heard Pep's familiar bark and Pa and Reuben calling our names.

"See what I told you?" I said to Sarah Jane.

She was so happy to see Pa and Reuben coming toward us, she didn't even answer me. Instead she jumped up, waving her hands in the air. "Over here, Mr. O'Dell."

Soon Pa was scooping me up in his arms, and I was on my way home.

That evening after the excitement was over, Ma bent down and hugged Pep.

"I guess you're good for something after all, old fellow," she said. "I won't doubt your intelligence again. And the next b-o-n-e you get will have some m-e-a-t on it!"

chapter twenty-six

The Surprise Birthday Present

I always loved birthday parties. Balloons. Games. Ice cream and cake. Attending them was such fun.

But before I could go, I had to buy the present with my own money. Somehow my allowance was always gone and I ended up explaining my problem to Grandma and asking her, "Can you think of any way I can earn some money?"

She never failed me. There was always some job to be done. But sometimes it took a long time.

"I need all this wool rolled into balls," Grandma replied one time I asked her to help me earn money. "Stretch the skein over the back of the chair, and I'll show you how to start."

"How many skeins are there?"

"Only about twelve." Grandma laughed. "Enough to keep you busy for a while."

"Can you tell me a story while I'm working?" I asked hopefully.

Grandma thought for a moment. "I guess I can tell you about a time I worked to earn some money. It wasn't as easy as rolling yarn, but it was for the same purpose."

"A birthday present? Whom was it for?"

"It was for Pa," Grandma replied. "The whole family went together to try to earn money for it. . . ."

🗒

PA'S BIRTHDAY WAS IN MAY, but we started thinking about it right after Christmas. We had attended a service at the church on New Year's Eve, and Ma remarked about the state of Pa's good suit.

"Your work overalls look better than your Sunday suit," she said to him. "The seat of those pants is so thin I don't think you're going to be able to wear them much longer."

"I agree that they aren't in the best of shape," Pa replied. "But I can't afford another suit this year. Maybe if the crops are good, I can get one next winter. In the meantime, I'll just sit easy."

Ma shook her head. "That one will never last. But I don't know what we can do about it."

Nothing further was said, but Ma didn't forget about Pa's worn suit. One morning in January she mentioned it again before we left for school.

"The new Sears catalog is here," she said. "We could get a good suit for your father for twenty-five dollars.

219

The question is, where will we get twenty-five dollars?"

"Twenty-five dollars!" I gasped. It might as well have been twenty-five thousand, as far as we were concerned.

"It would sure be nice to get that suit for his birthday," Ma continued. "I'm going to start thinking about how I can earn some money."

"We will, too," Reuben offered. "Roy and I can go in with you and buy it."

"I want to help, too," I put in. "I can earn money if you can."

Ma looked at me kindly. "There's not much a little girl can do for pay. But it's nice of you to offer. We'll see what we can do."

On the way to school that morning, I took up the matter with Sarah Jane.

"What would you do to earn a whole lot of money if you needed it?" I asked her.

Sarah Jane looked startled. "Do you need a whole lot of money?"

"Yes, I need twenty-five dollars."

She stopped short in the middle of the road and stared at me. "Twenty-five dollars!" she exclaimed. "You couldn't earn that much in a million years. What do you need it for?"

"You're not much help," I sighed. "I need it for a new suit for Pa. And I don't have a million years. I only have until May."

Sarah Jane counted on her fingers. "That's just five months away. You'll never make it. How come you have to buy your Pa a suit, anyway?"

"I don't actually have to do it all alone. But I want to earn my part. Ma and the boys don't think I can earn any money, but I'll show them."

"Well, good luck," Sarah Jane said. "If I think of some way, I'll let you know."

We walked the rest of the way in silence, but my mind was busy searching for ideas. I was only half listening as Miss Gibson read the Scripture for the morning.

"Trust in the Lord . . . wait patiently for Him . . . and He will give you the desires of your heart."

There was the answer! Trust in the Lord. I knew all about doing that. We had been taught that God takes care of his children and gives them everything that is necessary. A new suit for Pa was necessary, wasn't it?

But wait patiently? That would be the hard part. I wasn't very long on patience. I usually wanted things to happen right away—or sooner. I could just see that suit in the catalog.

"Mabel." Miss Gibson's voice broke into my thoughts.

"Yes?"

"I've spoken to you twice now. Where has

your mind been?"

"In the catalog," I blurted out, and then turned red as everyone laughed. "I mean, I was thinking about the Sears catalog. I'm sorry. I'll listen now."

At recess time, Miss Gibson came over to where Sarah Jane and I sat on the steps. "Did you see something in the catalog you wanted, Mabel?" she asked me.

"Yes, ma'am. I want a suit for my pa."

Miss Gibson looked thoughtful. "That's a pretty big order. Where will you get the money for it?"

"That's what I don't know," I replied. "But there must be something I could do to earn it."

Miss Gibson nodded. "I'm sure there is. You'll think of something."

All of January went by, and I had not earned a single penny. Reuben brought home ten cents he had earned helping a neighbor mend harnesses. Roy got five cents for sweeping out Mr. Clapp's store.

"He wanted to give me candy," Roy reported. "But I told him I needed the money."

Ma had sold some eggs, and made a dress for the minister's wife. Altogether she had a dollar and a half.

"A dollar and sixty-five cents," Reuben counted. "We're not getting there very fast, are we?"

"It's $1.65 more than we had at the beginning of the month," Ma reminded him. "We'll keep working and praying about it."

In February Mrs. Carter gave me a nickel for going to the store for her. I had to make three trips to get everything she wanted, but it was worth it. Joyfully I handed it over to Ma.

"That's good, Mabel. Every little bit helps. We have almost three dollars now. You mustn't be too disappointed if we can't earn it all. We'll do the best we can."

"But, Ma," I protested, "The Bible says if we trust in the Lord, He'll give us the desires of our heart. We're trusting Him, aren't we?"

"Yes, of course," Ma replied. "But remember, God doesn't always answer our prayers the way we expect him to. He gives us what is best for us. Money may not be His best."

I couldn't think of anything that would be better, but I didn't say that to Ma. Every so often when Pa was in the fields or the barn, I would take down the jar that held our savings and count it again.

"If you think that money will multiply because you count it every day, it won't," Roy advised me. "You'll just wear it out."

"I will not!" I retorted. "It doesn't hurt money to count it."

"Doesn't help it any, either," Roy teased.

March passed slowly, and then April arrived with heavy spring rains. After it had rained for two

Saturdays in a row, I complained to Ma.

"How can I go out and find errands to do in this kind of weather? It isn't good for anything."

"Except to help the gardens and fields to grow," Ma reminded me. "Nothing that God sends is useless."

The next week a rainstorm did help solve our problem. Sarah Jane and I were spending the afternoon at her house. Just as we had gathered all our things together to go to the creek to play, it began to rain.

"Oh, bother!" Sarah Jane exclaimed. "Now what shall we do?"

"Why don't you play in the attic?" her mother suggested. "You can use the clothes in the old trunk to play dress-up if you like."

"We can make up a story to go with it," I added. "Come on. That's much more fun than going to the creek."

We hurried to the attic and lost no time in selecting dresses and hats to try on. Sarah Jane even found an old pair of high-top shoes that just fit her.

"It's too bad your feet are so big, Mabel," she said smugly. "I guess I'll just have to wear these."

"That's all right," I replied. "I'll use the parasol. It's prettier anyway."

After prancing around the attic for a few minutes, another thought occurred to me.

"Maybe I can find some long gloves in there to go with my parasol."

After routing through a couple more dresses, I lifted out something heavy. It was made of a woolen material.

"Hey, look at this," I called. "What is it?"

Sarah Jane came over to look. "It was a great coat of my grandfather's."

"My, it's big," I marveled. "I never saw so much cloth in one coat."

"My grandpa was big," Sarah Jane informed me. "My mother said he would make two of anyone she ever saw. No one else has ever been able to wear his coat."

I could hardly get my breath for excitement. "Oh, Sarah Jane, do you think your mother would sell it to us?"

"Sell it to you? Whatever for? Your Pa could wrap it around him three times. He would sure look silly in it."

"No, no. He wouldn't wear it like that. Ma could make him a whole suit out of it! She can do anything with a needle and thread."

"We'll have to ask. Ma might want to sell it."

But she didn't. "Oh, my. I couldn't take money for an old coat like that. I can't imagine what anyone would want it for. But if you think your mother could use it, you may have it."

"Oh, thank you!" I cried. "I just know we can use it. I'll take it home right now."

"You'd better wait until it stops raining," Sarah Jane suggested. "Wet wool doesn't smell too good, you know."

She was right, so I waited impatiently for the weather to clear. Then Sarah Jane helped me roll the coat into a bundle I could carry.

I hurried as fast as I could, for the coat was really quite heavy. When I finally arrived at our yard, Pa was starting toward the house.

Quickly I detoured around to the barn and went in. The coat would be safe under some hay until after supper.

Ma watched me anxiously as we ate. "Aren't you hungry, Mabel?"

"No, not very."

"Your cheeks are flushed. Are you feverish?"

"I don't think so, Ma. I feel fine, really I do."

Fortunately, she said no more. As soon as we were alone doing the dishes, I whispered to her. "There's something in the barn you have to see, Ma. It's an answer to our prayer!"

Ma looked surprised, but she didn't question me. As soon as we were finished, we hurried out to the barn. I laid the big coat out on the straw for her to inspect.

"Sarah Jane and I found this in a trunk, Ma.

Her mother said we could have it. You can make a suit for Pa out of it, can't you?"

Ma was so astonished that she couldn't speak for a moment. "Why, Mabel, I believe I can! Isn't this wonderful? We can get buttons for it with the money we've saved. We'll even have enough money left over to buy a fine linen handkerchief."

Ma hugged me, and together we took the coat to the house.

"Monday we'll start taking the seams out," she said. "I'll brush the pieces good and air them. When they are pressed neatly, they'll be as fine as any yard goods. I do believe we can have it ready for Pa's birthday."

And it was. On the third Sunday in May, Pa proudly left for church in his new suit.

"I don't know where you got enough money to buy anything as nice as this," he said to us. "I didn't see one this fine in the catalog. You didn't sell one of the cows, did you?" he teased.

"Never mind, Pa," I said. "That's our secret. I can tell you this much, though. We trusted in the Lord, and waited patiently for Him. Then He gave us the desires of our heart!"

chapter twenty-seven

The Perfect Party

"We sure do have a nice teacher this year," I said to Grandma shortly after school had started in the fall. "I thought Mrs. Bingham was the best last year, but Mrs. Dorman is just as good."

"I'm glad," Grandma replied. "School is always so much nicer when you like your teacher. I never had the experience of changing teachers every year. Ours usually stayed five or six years or more."

"Was Miss Gibson your favorite one?" I asked. "You've told me a lot of stories about her."

"Yes. I think she probably was. She certainly had a lot of patience to put up with all the foolishness we got into.

"We always looked for things to take to her—or something to surprise her with. But we were pretty limited in our offerings. There wasn't money to buy things, so we had to use our imaginations. . . .

THE SECOND YEAR MISS GIBSON was our
teacher, Sarah Jane and I were in the third reader.
The school wasn't large that year, only about 15
students. But we all loved Miss Gibson.

One day the sixth-reader class was reciting at
the front of the room. As usual Sarah Jane and I
listened in.

"Shakespeare was born in 1564," Miss Gibson
told them. "There is some argument about the
day. Some people say April 23 and some say April
26. I would like to think it is April 23, because
that's the day I was born. I'd like to share a
birthday with a famous person. But it's probably
April 26."

At recess time, Sarah Jane and I discussed what
we had overheard.

"Now that we know the date, we should plan a
big birthday party for Miss Gibson," I suggested.
"Don't you think that would be fun?"

"Oh, yes," Sarah Jane agreed. "I won't forget
her birthday, either, because Caleb's is April 26.
Maybe he shares a birthday with Shakespeare. It
depends on who's right about the date."

"I think we should let Miss Gibson have it."

Sarah Jane nodded. "I think so, too. Caleb
wouldn't care if Shakespeare had been born right

on our own farm, let alone on his birthday. Where shall we have the party?"

"If we're going to invite a lot of people, we'd better have it here. There are fifteen of us in school. We'll all bring our families so that will be a big crowd."

"That's a good idea," Sarah Jane said. "We can decorate the room with streamers and all the spring flowers we can find."

"And we'll make a big banner that says 'Happy Birthday, Miss Gibson.' Won't she be surprised?"

"She will if we can keep the little kids from telling her. We'll have to threaten them with a thump on the head if they tell."

"We can't do that," I argued. "I think they'll keep the secret when we let them know how important it is. The first time Miss Gibson is out of the room, we'll announce it."

Our chance came that afternoon. We were studying quietly when Miss Gibson stood up. "Children, I've just found that I left some of your papers at home. While you're working, I'll go back and get them. I shouldn't be more than a few minutes, so you are on your honor."

As soon as the door closed and we were sure Miss Gibson was out of hearing, Sarah Jane jumped to her feet.

"Listen, everyone. We want to have a surprise

party here at school for Miss Gibson on her birthday. If someone in each family bakes a cake, we should have plenty. I think my folks and Mabel's will make the ice cream. It will be at seven o'clock in the evening on April 23. Don't forget the date. And whatever you do, don't let Miss Gibson know about it!"

Sarah Jane fixed her eyes on the front row of beginners. "It's a secret. Do you promise you won't tell?"

They nodded solemnly.

"All right. We'll talk later about decorating the room. Remember, not a word!"

She sat back down. By the time Miss Gibson returned, everyone was working quietly. On the way home after school, Sarah Jane and I continued our plans.

"I'm not worried about the cake and ice cream, but what are we going to give her?" I asked. "I don't have any money to get anything, do you?"

Sarah Jane shook her head. "I never have any money. Do you suppose we should ask our folks for some?"

"I don't think so. These should be our gifts to Miss Gibson. Besides," I added, "Pa doesn't have any money for things like presents. I'm sure we can think of something to make her."

That night at supper, I brought up the subject.

"It's going to be a wonderful party," I told Ma and Pa. "Miss Gibson will be so pleased. And it's really going to be a surprise. But I have to decide on a present. What do you think I could do, Ma?"

"I know what I'm going to do," Roy put in. "I'll give her the bookends I'm carving."

"That will make a nice gift," Ma said. "Mabel, how would you like to make a pretty apron? I'll cut it out for you if you want to stitch it."

"Oh, yes, Ma! She'll like that. Do you think I can get it done in two weeks?"

"I'm sure you can if you work on it after school every day. We'll start this evening. How about you, Reuben? Do you have an idea for a gift?"

"Do you remember the picture of the schoolhouse I drew? Do you think that would be all right?"

"I think that would be just the thing," Pa said. "Get it out, and I'll help you frame it."

On the way to school the following morning, Sarah Jane and I compared notes.

"The apron is all ready to start sewing on," I said. "I'll begin as soon as I get home. What are you going to make?"

"I wanted to do a sampler for her, but Ma thinks that will take too long. I can't think of anything else to do."

"Why don't you hemstitch some towels? They would go nicely with the apron."

"I don't know how to hemstitch!" Sarah Jane exclaimed. "If I learned on Miss Gibson's towels, it wouldn't be a very pretty present."

"Just put a plain hem, then. You already know how to embroider. You could put her initials on them."

"That sounds good. Let's hurry home as soon as we can and get started."

For the next week I worked every afternoon on the apron. Some days Sarah Jane brought her towels over, and we talked as we sat on the porch steps sewing.

"This is one thing we've planned that isn't going to go wrong," she declared. "I can't think of a thing we've left out, can you?"

"Not a thing," I said. "And for once I haven't even had to take my sewing out. This time everything is going to be perfect."

"Would you girls like some cookies?" Ma called through the screen door. "I'm taking fresh ones from the oven."

"Oh, yes, Ma! I'll come right in and get them." I picked up the apron to put it aside but it would not move. It was sewn to my pinafore!

Sarah Jane looked at it; then she burst out laughing.

"I'm sure I don't know what's funny," I said crossly. "Would you want me to laugh if you did that?"

"I'm sorry, Mabel. But you just finished saying that you hadn't taken any stitches out yet. And I said that nothing was going to go wrong. I guess we were both mistaken, weren't we?"

Ma appeared in the doorway to see what had happened. "I wouldn't say that it would be safe for either one of you to boast about anything being perfect," she commented. "I've seen things that couldn't possibly go wrong, fall apart when you two got mixed up in them."

She pointed to the apron on my lap. "If taking out a little sewing is the worst that happens, you won't have to worry."

"It had better be the worst," I grumbled. "I don't have the time to be doing things over."

It was a good thing that we couldn't see the future. The Bible is right when it says that each day's troubles are enough for that day. We don't need to know that more will follow.

Everything went well until April 23, the day of the party. If Miss Gibson noticed that her class seemed more restless that day, she didn't mention it. But for most of us, it was the longest day of the year.

At closing time, Reuben raised his hand. "A

couple of us would like to stay and work a little longer, Miss Gibson. I'll be sure to lock up if it's all right."

"Why, that's fine, boys,'" she replied. "I'm glad to see you so interested in your studies. I'll be happy to stay awhile, too, if you like."

We held our breath.

"Oh, no thank you, Miss Gibson. We'll get along just fine," Reuben answered her. "You can go right along home."

Fortunately, she agreed. When school was dismissed, most of us left the yard as she did. But when she was out of sight, we returned quickly.

"We'll put two tables together at the front to hold the presents," Reuben directed. "The cakes can go on the desks by the wall. Now let's hurry and put the streamers around."

Miss Gibson's desk was chosen as the ideal place for the happy birthday banner. Sarah Jane and I set to work at once to print it.

"Be sure you don't spell something wrong, Mabel," Roy called. "You've got four whole words to put on there."

"Ignore him," I told Sarah Jane. "He thinks he's so bright. He'd like you to believe that he'd never made a mistake in his life."

When we were finished, Reuben locked the

door, and we hurried home to get ready for the party.

"Try to get your folks to leave a little bit early," Sarah Jane said. "Then we can be there to welcome everyone."

I assured her that we would be there by quarter of seven, and we were. By seven o'clock the others began to arrive. We hurried about, placing cakes and gifts in their proper places.

Soon the room began to fill up. Whenever the door opened, we looked expectantly toward it. But Miss Gibson did not appear.

"Do you suppose we should go and get her?" Sarah Jane asked me. "Or at least go over and see when she's coming?"

I agreed that we should and we ran across the school ground to the minister's home, where Miss Gibson lived.

"But she's not here," the minister's wife told us when we inquired about Miss Gibson. "Her parents came and took her into town for dinner."

"Everyone is here for her birthday party!" I cried.

"Mabel," Sarah Jane said, "did you tell her about the party?"

We looked at each other in silence.

"You didn't tell her, either," I said. "Nobody told her. What do we do now?"

"I'll tell her," offered Mrs. Brooke. "As soon as she gets home I'll send her right over there. Why don't you just go ahead with your party?"

There was nothing else to do. Slowly we went back to the school.

"You'd think we'd learn, wouldn't you?" Sarah Jane said sadly. "We can't even have a party that goes right. What are we going to tell them?"

"We'll just have to say that everyone kept the secret so well that Miss Gibson still doesn't know it. . . . I hope she gets back early."

Happily, Miss Gibson and her parents arrived at eight o'clock. The party was a huge success, and she was greatly pleased with her gifts.

When she thanked us, she said, "It isn't often that a surprise party is a surprise to the people who give it!"

"No," Pa agreed, "not unless it's Sarah Jane and Mabel who are giving it. Then anything can happen!"

chapter twenty-eight

Revenge

"MA, DO YOU KNOW where my cameo pin is? It was in my room this morning, and now it's gone."

Ma shook her head. "I haven't seen it, Mabel. Are you sure you know where you left it?"

"I'm sure," I replied. "I was trying to fix the clasp when it was time to leave for school, and I didn't bother to put it back in the drawer. It was on top of the table."

Ma looked doubtful. "You've misplaced things before," she said. "I know you think you remember, but perhaps you don't."

"But I do!" I insisted. "If that Roy has taken my pin, he's going to be sorry!"

"Now, don't accuse your brother without any more evidence than that," Ma cautioned. "It could have fallen off the table, or you may have slid something on top of it."

I was sure that wasn't the case, but I went back

to look again. A thorough search of the room revealed no cameo. When Roy came in for dinner, I lost no time approaching him on the subject.

Roy looked surprised; then he grinned.

"If I did something like that, do you think I'd tell you about it?" he teased.

"You see, Ma? He doesn't deny it!"

Ma sighed. "He hasn't admitted it, either," she replied. "Roy, I'll be glad when you're old enough not to torment your sister."

"He'll never live that long," I retorted. "He doesn't know how to do anything but torment me."

A few days later, a small comb with shiny stones in the top was missing.

"It's too bad if I can't leave something on my own table in my own room without Roy meddling with it," I stormed. "Ma, can't you do something about him?"

Ma questioned Roy. "How come I get blamed for everything?" he asked. "I'm only one-fifth of the family. And not the most irresponsible fifth at that," he added, looking at me.

"I've never taken anything out of his room just to be mean," I said to Ma after he had left. "He's the one who thinks of tricks like that."

"I don't like these accusations, Mabel," Ma interrupted. "You have no proof that Roy has taken any of your things."

"But he never says he didn't," I wailed. "Nobody makes him own up to anything."

"We'll not discuss it further," Ma said firmly. "You put your things where they belong and they'll not disappear."

I felt the situation was grossly unfair, but I knew better than to say any more. Instead I glared at Roy when he came back in. If he didn't know what I was glaring about, he at least had the good sense not to ask.

About a week before Ma's birthday, Pa gave me a shiny new quarter to add to what I had saved for her gift.

"What are you going to get for her?" Sarah Jane asked me. "How much money do you have?"

"I'm going to open my bank this afternoon and see what I have. I'd like to get that new brush and comb set at the general store, if I can afford it. Don't you think she'd like that?"

"I'm sure she would," Sarah Jane replied. "Will you get the silver or the tortoise shell?"

"They're both so pretty, I can't decide," I answered. "Let's look at them together on Saturday. You can tell me which you like best."

After school I went directly to my room and emptied my bank out on the table. One dollar and twenty-eight cents. With the quarter Pa had given me, there would be enough for Ma's present and three cents left over.

Just then Ma called from the kitchen. "I forgot to bring in the last of the eggs, Mabel. Would you please go out to the barn and get them?"

When I got back, I helped myself to the cookies she was taking from the oven.

"I guess one won't spoil your supper," she said. "Sit down and tell me how your history report went today."

It was soon time to set the table, eat supper, and help with the dishes. I didn't get back to my room until after family prayer.

As I scooped up my money to put it back in the bank, I saw at once that the quarter was gone. I started to call Ma, and then realized that I couldn't tell her about the quarter. I'd take care of this myself.

"I'll get even with Roy if it's the last thing I do," I declared to Sarah Jane the next morning. "He'll be sorry he ever had me for a sister."

"I think that's already the case," Sarah Jane said. "But what makes you so sure Roy took all those things? I know he can be a pest, but he wouldn't steal."

"He wouldn't call it stealing—he'd call it hiding things someplace else just to make you look for them," I replied. "He needs a lesson he won't forget for a while."

"What are you going to do?"

"I don't know yet. You'll have to help me think of something."

"Me?" Sarah Jane exclaimed. "How did I get in on this?"

"You're my best friend. As you always say, 'What are best friends for?' "

The day passed slowly. I found myself reading a page several times before I knew what it said, because my mind wandered to the problem of what I could do to get back at Roy.

"Come and see the new kittens we have," I said to Sarah Jane on the way home. "Two calicos and a tabby."

As we approached the barn, we could hear Roy sneezing. He met with us at the door with tears running down his face.

"You sure got a noseful of something," Sarah Jane said. "What was it?"

"That patch of weeds beside the barn," Roy wheezed. "I forgot I was so allergic to them and waded right though it." He sneezed again. "I'll get over it if I stay away from there."

He went over to the pump to splash water on his face, and Sarah Jane pulled me into the barn.

"There's your answer," she said.

"What's the question?"

"What you can do to get even with Roy," she explained. "If he spent a night sleeping on those weeds, he'd repent in a hurry."

"What are you thinking of?" I asked. "How could I get Roy to sleep in a weed patch?"

"Of course you couldn't, silly. I was thinking of bringing the weed patch to him. Stuff some of them in his pillowcase."

I stared at Sarah Jane in admiration.

"Of course!" I exclaimed. "It would serve him right if he sneezed all night. I'll do it!"

At suppertime, Pa made an announcement. "I'm going over to the county seat tomorrow morning to file some papers. How would you all like to go with me?"

Ma's face brightened. "Why, how nice," she said. "We can take a picnic lunch and maybe even stop and see Harriet and Wesley Blake on the way home. We haven't had an outing like that for a long time."

Roy was excited. "That will be great, Pa. Do you think we'll have time to visit the horse barns at the fairgrounds?"

"I don't see why not," Pa replied. "We'll start early and make a whole day of it."

While we cleared away the dishes, Ma and I talked happily about what we would do the next day. "I think I'll get to bed early so I can get up and help you with the lunch," I said.

"That will be nice, Mabel," Ma said, hugging me. "I'm thankful for such a good daughter."

She might have changed her mind if she had known what her good daughter was up to. I brought in two large handfuls of weeds and pushed them into Roy's pillowcase.

Several times that night I awoke to hear Roy sneezing. Once I heard Ma's voice as she spoke to him. *He had it coming*, I thought with satisfaction. *He'll learn to keep his hands off my things*.

Before daylight I heard Ma stirring, and I hurried to dress so that I could help her. We were putting things into the picnic basket when Roy came into the kitchen.

"Oh, Roy!" Ma gasped. "Whatever has happened to you?"

Poor Roy was hardly able to get his breath. His face was swollen, and his eyes were practically closed. Between wheezes he managed to tell Ma about the weeds.

"I guess I got more than I thought yesterday. I think they've poisoned me."

"Oh, dear," Ma said. "You're in no condition for a trip. I'll fix you some honeycomb and lemon and see if we can take care of it."

I was appalled. I had meant to teach Roy a lesson, not kill him. He would be furious when he found out what I had done. I decided not to tell him. I'd shake out his pillow and put a clean case on it. He didn't have to know I was to blame for his sorry state.

"I can't leave Roy alone like this," Ma said as we ate breakfast. "You and Mabel and Reuben go ahead and enjoy the day."

Needless to say, I didn't. The look on Roy's face as we drove off, and the knowledge that Ma was missing the fun, too, cancelled any joy I might have had in the trip.

"I suffered as much as Roy did," I told Sarah Jane the next day. "I guess that will teach me to believe what the Bible says about vengeance belonging to the Lord."

"Are you going to ask him to forgive you?" Sarah Jane wanted to know.

"Are you out of your mind? He'd clobber me!"

"You know what the Bible says about forgiveness," Sarah Jane shrugged. "I wouldn't want to live with that on my conscience."

"It should be on your conscience," I retorted. "It was your idea. I don't know why I always end up being the guilty party."

But in spite of my conscience, I didn't tell Roy what I had done. I pushed it to the back of my mind and, as the weeks went by, I forgot about it. One morning in the fall, Pa called Roy to the yard.

"There's a branch right over Mabel's window that needs cutting off," he said. "The first big wind could bring it down on the roof."

Roy got the ladder and the saw and prepared to do the job. A few minutes later, I heard him call.

"Mabel! Come here and see this!" He held out a large bird's nest. Inside lay my pin, my comb, and a shiny quarter.

"A magpie's nest," Roy said. "They're the worst thieves in the world—grab anything that shines. You must have had your window open."

"I did," I said, and I began to cry.

"Girls!" Roy said in disgust. "I thought you'd be glad to see this stuff. I'll put it back up there if you want me to."

Between sobs I managed to tell Roy what I had done and ask him to forgive me.

"I ought to smack you good," he told me. "But I guess you feel bad enough already."

"Do we have to tell Pa and Ma?" I asked.

"I don't," Roy replied. "It's up to you."

"Did they punish you?" Sarah Jane asked later, when I told her what had happened.

"Not in the regular way," I replied. "They felt so bad about it that it made me feel worse. I'm sure Pa's way of loving people instead of getting even with them is the best."

"I don't know why you can't remember that," Sarah Jane said with a sigh. "It would certainly save you a lot of heartache."

"You should be pounded," I told her. "I wonder if anyone else ever had a best friend like you."

chapter twenty-nine

Monday's Child

"MA, ON WHAT DAY of the week was I born?"

"Monday," Ma replied. "You started the week out for us. Pa had to finish the washing that day."

"Monday's child is fair of face," I quoted. "Do you think I'm fair of face?"

"That's a poem, not a promise," Ma said. "Beauty is as beauty does."

"Do you really think people's looks depend on what they do?" I asked.

Ma thought for a moment. "I think it means that your actions show what you are like inside. You can be a beautiful person even without having a pretty face. I've known people who spoiled their good looks by being selfish and inconsiderate."

"I guess that means you don't think I'm fair of face, so I'd better be good to make up for it."

Ma laughed. "You're beautiful to me, Mabel. And

it certainly doesn't hurt to be good and fair of face."

"Would you rather be good or beautiful?" I asked Sarah Jane when I saw her.

"How could you make a choice like that?" she replied. "I'd like to be beautiful, but I don't want to be bad. On the other hand, I'd like to be good, but I don't want to be ugly. It's like asking if I'd rather keep my eyes or my ears. I need both."

"It was just a simple question," I sighed. "Why do I hear a lecture every time I ask you something?"

"Because there is usually something to be said on both sides of everything," Sarah Jane replied. "What did you ask me the question for?"

"I thought I wanted to know," I said. "What day of the week were you born on?"

"Friday. What's that got to do with being beautiful or good?"

"Miss Gibson gave me a poem to copy from one of her books. It says:

Monday's child is fair of face.
Tuesday's child is full of grace.
Wednesday's child is full of woe.
Thursday's child has far to go.
Friday's child is loving and giving.
Saturday's child must work for a living.
The child that's born on the Sabbath day
is bonnie and blithe and good always.

"I'd say that's a pretty fair description of Friday's child," Sarah Jane nodded. "What's your day?"

"Monday—fair of face."

"I suppose it can't be right every time," she said with a grin.

"That's what Ma thought, too. She told me that beauty is as beauty does. Do you think that's true?"

"I don't know," Sarah Jane shrugged. "Why don't you try it and find out?"

"Try what?"

"Being good. See if it makes you beautiful."

"I am good!" I protested. "I don't think I'm a bad person."

"I'd agree with that." Sarah Jane eyed me carefully. "There are a few notable exceptions, but I'd say you come in with the best. But maybe some extra good deeds would help. What would you like to do for me?"

"Come over to study this evening and I'll help you with your arithmetic," I told her. "Will that be good enough?"

Sarah Jane nodded and turned toward home.

"You're the one that's loving and giving." I called after her. "What are you going to bring me?"

"My pleasant, amiable self," she called back.

Ma and I had almost finished the supper dishes when Sarah Jane came in and plopped her books on the table.

"You go ahead," I said to Ma. "I can finish here. Go sit with Pa on the porch."

"Well, thank you, Mabel," Ma said gratefully. "It will feel good to rest a bit. Be sure you cover the pitcher of milk in the pantry."

"I will," I promised. I finished washing out the dish towels and hung them up. Then I stopped to look at the art project Sarah Jane was working on. We talked about it for several minutes when she reminded me about the milk.

I went to cover it. "Too late. There's a fly in it." I carried the pitcher to the table and set it down. "I'm not going to lose this whole pitcher of milk— come and help me."

"What are you going to do?" Sarah Jane asked.

"Why, strain it out, of course. Here, you hold the strainer over the sink."

Sarah Jane obeyed and I quickly poured out the milk. She watched in fascination as the milk went down the sink and she was left with a very dead fly in the bottom of the strainer.

"Mabel, you are the only person in the world who could do a thing like that. Now what are you going to do with the fly, frame it?"

"I should have put a pan under it," I said lamely. "I just thought it was a shame to waste all that milk."

Sarah Jane shook her head. "Did you ever

think of just skimming the fly off the top? Though I don't imagine your ma would want it, anyway, after it had a fly in it."

"That's what I get for trying to be helpful," I said. "I should have been a Wednesday's child."

"If that's an example of the good deeds you have planned, you can say good-bye to your beauty," Sarah Jane predicted.

"Oh, be quiet and sit down," I told her. "If you want help with your arithmetic, forget the smart remarks."

"I'm sorry, Mabel. It's just that the sight of that fly in the bottom of the strainer . . . ."

"Sarah Jane!" I began, and then the ridiculous situation hit me, too, and I began to laugh. Sarah Jane joined in. We laughed so hard that Ma looked in to see what was going on.

"I don't remember arithmetic being that amusing," she said. "That is what you're doing, isn't it?"

We tried to concentrate on our lessons for the rest of the evening.

"Why is it that the good things I try to do most always turn out wrong?" I asked Ma later. "If I can't be good or fair of face, I might as well give up."

"I understand how you feel," Ma answered. "But just remember that when you have a choice between right and wrong, and with the Lord's help you choose to do right, you are becoming a beautiful person."

Ma's words were comforting, but I wasn't convinced that the best kind of beauty was on the inside. I wanted to be pretty on the outside, too.

On Saturday, Sarah Jane and I were looking through the general store, as we usually did. There was always the possibility that something new had come in since the last Saturday. Suddenly Sarah Jane clutched my arm.

"Look—over there by the door. Now there is a real Monday's child!"

I nodded in agreement. The girl who stood there was truly as beautiful as anyone we had ever seen. She had perfect features, and her smile seemed to light up the store.

"Did you ever see such long eyelashes?" Sarah Jane whispered. "And look at that wavy hair."

We were not the only ones admiring the young lady. Several young men were gathered around talking with her, and people walking by cast appreciative glances in her direction.

"I wouldn't ever ask for anything else if I could look like that," I sighed. "Just think how happy she must be."

At that moment an older woman approached the group by the door. "Come, Hannah," she said.

"It's time to leave. Pa is waiting for us."

The smile disappeared from the girl's face, and she frowned at her mother.

"I'm not ready yet. Pa can just wait."

"Now don't be difficult," her mother admonished. "You know we have to be home before dark."

The girl's look was stubborn, and she turned her back on the woman.

"I'll come when I'm ready. You do nothing but nag at me. You don't care whether I have a good time or not." Her angry voice carried throughout the store, and Sarah Jane and I looked at each other in wonder.

"Why does her ma let get away with that?" I wondered.

"Maybe because she's older," Sarah Jane suggested. "She must be seventeen or eighteen."

"I wouldn't answer my ma like that if I were a hundred and seventeen," I declared. "I don't think that girl is as pretty as she looks."

Suddenly Ma's words came back to me. "I've known people who spoiled their good looks by being selfish and inconsiderate."

"You know," I said to Sarah Jane, "Ma was right about beauty. If it's just on your face, you can ruin it with what you do."

"I'm glad you've realized that," Sarah Jane said.

"Now you can stop worrying about how you look and concentrate on being a better person. There is always room for improvement, you know, and you seem to have more room than most people. Fortunately, I'll always be around to help when you need it . . . ."

I walked away and left Sarah Jane talking to herself; I'd heard it all before. It wasn't every girl who had two consciences to live with . . . but I wouldn't give up Sarah Jane for anything in the world.